INVISIBLE  ENEMIES

by Bill Muir

Invisible Enemies

Bill Muir

Methinx Publishing

MeThinx Publishing

Methinx Publishing
methinxentertainment.com

Printed in the United States of America
First paper edition by Methinx Publishing
ISBN: 978-1-7347696-7-8

Art & Design:
Contributing Editor: Kathryn Tedrick
Cover Art: Digital Coast Media, LLC

Prologue

Rain poured from the dark gray sky that September day in 1888. Located on a cobblestone street in the thriving business district of Boston was a small shop with a wooden sign hanging over the front door. Chiseled into the wood was a sculpture of a pair of eyeglasses and the words Since 1854. In the workshop, behind the customer area of the store, Dr. George Alexander, a stout, medium height man with a ring of light brown hair that circled his bald head and blue eyes, worked on a new pair of glasses. He had already ground the left lens and laid it on a soft cloth on his workbench.

As he worked on the right lens, George whistled a popular tune. A second-generation optometrist, he had followed in his father's footsteps.

Working carefully, he ground the lens to fit the prescription. He then placed both lenses in rimless frames. As he looked at the lens, his trained eye noticed the angles were askew. Before taking the lenses out of the frame to start all over, he raised the glasses to his eyes. As he did, he heard voices. Puzzled, he stopped and looked around. No one else was in the room. Again, he raised the glasses, and the voices became louder. He looked around again, no one. He shook his head and blinked.

Raising the glasses a third time, he placed them on the bridge of his rather large nose. The lenses immediately turned dark, and what he saw made his pupils dilate in shock. The room and its belongings were blurred and double-layered. His head started to pound as he squinted and peered around the chamber, trying to focus through the odd lenses. The air heavy in the room, movement to his right demanded that he look. He clutched at the worktable. Never had he come upon anything like this, two beings. Not people, but evil creatures, ugly beyond description, and more than that, they exuded

3

crassness, anger, perversion, and toxic emotion seemed to fill the very air George breathed.

Demons. He knew. They were demons from the very pit of hell.

The demons stood by the workbench laughing in loud guffaws that grated against his nerves. They ignored George as if they did not see him. Perhaps they didn't. He could only hope. The optometrist's hand shook violently, and he held his breath as he lowered the glasses. When he did, the horrific sight and the grating sound stopped.

Shocked by what he had just seen, George backed up blindly, knocking over equipment and stumbling over his own feet. Terror filled him, clenching his heart as if it would squeeze it to a pulp.

"No. No. This isn't possible!" He stared at the glasses on the workbench, where he had dropped them. His eyes fearfully searched the lab. Nothing. He was alone. Nothing else or no one else was there, but the terror still gripped him, and he knew, without a doubt, he was not alone.

Gingerly, he picked up the glasses and held them at arm's length so he could see through the lenses, but his hand began shaking so violently that he could hardly see at all. Then in all the double-layered images, he saw the demons, and every cell in his frail human body screamed silently in terror. He had been touched by their evil, and there was no reversal.

George flung the spectacles into the open fireplace and darted out of the shop and into the street as if the hounds of hell were on his heels.

He stood in the middle of the busy cobblestone street, horses and carts weaving to avoid him. He looked back at the front of his shop, wondering what evil he had released.

He tried to pray, but not being a man of much faith, he could not even conjure the words to express his fear or to ask for help. He wished only to have the memory of this terrible experience erased.

Wagon drivers yelled at him to get out of the road. Stiffly he walked to the wooden porch and stood there shaking as other store owners scurried by.

"George, you look like you have seen a ghost."

"George, you're as white as a sheet."

George stared at the front entrance of his store. He slowly opened the door and made his way to the fireplace. The glasses were lying there on the hearth, untouched by the flames.

He scanned the room, then quickly, with just two fingers, picked up the glasses and dropped them on the workbench. Nothing. Silence. He reached for a cloth and quickly wrapped it around-and-around the glasses. Unsatisfied, his eyes darted around the room until he found a small metal box with a lock and key. Carrying it to the bench, he carefully laid the wrapped glasses inside and slammed the lid, locking it securely. It was the best he could do. Perhaps with the glasses out of sight and locked up forever, he could forget.

Nevertheless, what should he do now? He had to hide them, make them disappear. But no matter where he looked, he couldn't find a secure hiding place. Carrying the box, he searched from room to room. Nothing. He looked up the stairs that led to the family quarters above and shook his head. Not there, it must be away from his family. Perhaps he should bury them, but people might wonder what he was burying and why.

A log shifted, the fire crackled, and George jumped. There…in the fireplace would be ideal, but not in the fire. He had already witnessed that neither the flames nor the heat destroyed the glasses. No, he had a better idea. He grabbed a hammer and chisel from his workbench and began scraping the mortar between the bricks.

George carefully removed two of the bricks on the lower left-hand side of the fireplace near the floor. The space was just large enough for the box. He shoved it inside and replaced the bricks. When he was finished, it was impossible to tell what he had done.

Satisfied, George stood up and asked God to protect him, ending with, "and may this evil never see the light of day again.

Chapter One

Routine

The Empty Cup had a long wooden counter with a glass case with three shelves featuring pastries, bagels, and cupcakes. Centered on the wall behind was a sign with three sections offering the menu selections, including hot drinks like flavored coffees, teas, cappuccinos, lattes, and hot chocolate, as well as iced drinks, frozen drinks, and special requests. Scattered about the room were several tall round tables with brown metal ladder-back chairs. People from various walks of life occupied many of the tables.

Dr. Jonathan R. Rickner, a 45-years-old, 5'11" tall man with a medium build, chestnut brown hair, and hazel eyes, stood in line watching the customers interact with each other. As the line inched forward, he found himself standing beside a table with a young woman reading *The Screwtape Letters* by C.S. Lewis.

"Enjoying the book?" Jon asked her.

"Um-hmm." She kept her eyes on the book, clearly not liking the interruption.

"You don't want to talk. Do you?"

"What? Are you a mind reader?" She asked, annoyed.

"No, a psychiatrist, almost the same thing."

She looked up at him with a little smile, enjoying his self-deprecating humor.

"Interesting idea, if you believe in that kind of thing," he said, referring to her book.

"What? You don't believe in the spirit world?"

"Hey, I'm a psychiatrist. I don't believe in a lot of things."

She loosened up. "Yeah, you are *really* messed up."

"Great diagnosis."

They both laughed.

When the young lady in front of him finished her order, Jon moved up to the next barista, a fresh-faced young man who loved classic rock and video games.

"Hey, Jon, regular order?"

"Morning, Mark, yep, just change that raspberry to a cheese Danish."

"Whoa, living on the edge today. You got it."

As Jon and several others waited for coffee, he glanced around the room again. Two college students were having a lively debate over an upcoming physics exam, and a woman in her thirties chatted with a friend on her cell phone. He listened briefly to her conversation about children and daycare before turning back toward the counter, spotting a new ceramic statuette of three monkeys sitting side-by-side. One covering his eyes with his hands, another one covering his ears, and the third covering his ears. Written on the base of the statuette were two words, *No Evil.* The meaning barely registered in his consciousness; they were just words.

"Here's your order, Jon. Carpe diem, my friend."

Jon lifted the two coffees and a small white bag with the Danish. "With this double latte, I am now armed to fight the battle."

"Be brave," replied Mark with a large smile.

Jon left the shop and took a cautious sip of his coffee as he walked down the street at a leisurely pace. His office was a block away, and as he strolled along the sidewalk, he smiled and nodded hello to several folks, receiving their greeting in return.

Down to earth and good-natured, his easy demeanor made it easy for folks to trust him, which helped make him useful as a counselor.

Walking up the steps to his office, he stopped by a sitting hunchbacked, 46-year-old homeless man. He was dressed in a functional pair of dark blue chinos that didn't quite reach the tops of his faded black canvas slip-on shoes, and a brown-checked shirt with a blue sports coat that he had received during his latest trip to Goodwill. Known only as Phil, his face was oval with a network of lines like a dried lakebed. He had a thin grey and white mustache and goatee that encircled his mouth. This was Phil's regular spot, and every workday morning, Jon brought him coffee and fresh Danish.

"Morning, Phil," Jon greeted him, handing him the other coffee and the Danish.

"Morning, Jon." Phil took the bag with the pastry first and opened the paper wrapped around it. "What's this? A cheese pastry?"

"I thought you might like something different for a change. You know, other than the same old, same old."

Phil shook his head. "Not me. I like the same thing every day. I'm a creature of habit."

"Okay, I'll remember that. Raspberry it is."

The homeless man started to wrap up the pastry but stopped and looked closely at it. He blinked and smiled, holding it up for Jon to see and pointing at it. "Lookie here…a figure of an angel!" He said, pointing to the surface.

Jon stared at it, searching, but it was evident by the expression on his face that all he saw was a pastry.

"Just as clear as can be," Phil insisted. "The outline of an angel. See there? I could never eat an angel, cheese, or raspberry."

He handed the Danish back to Jon, who peered at it again, but still saw nothing, so he wrapped it up and placed it back in the bag.

"Phil, any time you would like to talk…"

"We're talking now."

"I mean, you know…about why you are here."

"I know why I'm here," Phil replied.

"All right, I just wanted you to know that I am available. You know, if you ever want to talk. Any time. No charge. Just come on in."

"I'm here because I need to be here," Phil assured him. "No other reason."

"Okay, then. See you tomorrow."

Jon turned and started into the building.

"Hey, Jon!"

Jon stopped and turned around to face him.

"Tomorrow, raspberry, like usual. And Jon…have a good day!"

Jon held up his coffee in a toast. "To the battle."

Phil smiled and help up his coffee. "to the battle."

****

Jon's office was an older midsize, attractive house converted to an office fifteen years ago when Jon and his partner, Tom Peneles, bought it for their practice. Sitting close to the sidewalk, it had a small deep porch, five steps above ground level. Inside, the mid-sized reception area had a contemporary, but warm look with well-maintained oak floors. Behind a sliding window was an oversized maple reception desk with a beautiful scenic painting hanging on the wall behind it. Two love seats, an eight-foot couch, and three comfortable high-backed chairs, all in complementary warm fabrics filled the waiting area along with three coffee tables with various magazines ranging from *Sports Illustrated* to *Psychology Today*. A large, beautifully refinished armoire stood along one wall.

Across from the armoire was a large screen TV mounted on the wall. The volume was turned down, but still, one could hear it if seated close by. The windows to the street were large, and light streamed into the area.

Jon stopped at the receptionist's desk.

"How's Phil?" Vivian Newberry asked, her sky-blue eyes dancing with good humor.

Jon handed her the rejected pastry. "Apparently, he doesn't like cheese Danish."

"Ooo, my favorite, thank you, Phil." Reaching inside the bag, she removed the pastry and unwrapped it.

She was about to take a healthy bite when Jon said, "You may want to eat around the image of the angel."

Vivian held the pastry up to the light and carefully examined it. She did not see the image any more than Jon had, but she nibbled on a corner just to be sure. Following the bite, she rolled her eyes towards Jon's open office door.

"New client. A file's on your desk. His name is Carson Anderson."

Jon nodded and headed down the hallway to the left that led to his and Tom's offices. Walking into the first room on the left and closing the door, he entered his office.

It looked more like a living room with three chairs around a coffee table and a small desk tucked into a corner. White floor to ceiling bookshelves ran along one wall, and a uniquely framed large photo of a mountain trail hung on the other. Deep, Wedgewood blue carpeting covered the hardwood floor that matched the drapes and lighter shade of blue on the wall.

In one of the chairs sat a good-looking, well-dressed professional man. At first glance, he seemed well to do and normal, but closer inspection revealed a sweaty, anxious man with a haunted look on his face.

Walking over to him, Jon extended his hand. "Hello, Carson, I'm Jon."

Carson shook his hand briefly. "Hi."

Attempting to put the man at ease, Jon sat on a chair across from him. "Since this is your first visit, tell me a little about yourself and what you hope I can do for you."

Carson reached into his suit jacket and pulled out a pair of old rimless eyeglasses. "I see things when I wear these glasses."

Surprised by his jumping right in and stating the problem, Jon decided to go with it, as his patient appeared anxious.

"What kind of things?"

"Beings," Carson replied bluntly.

"People, you know?"

"Oh, no…not people."

"But they are beings."

"They're evil!" Carson blurted out. He held out the glasses. Not only his hand, but his entire body visibly shaking. "I believe they're demons."

Chapter Two

The Glasses

Carson stood up and advanced toward Jon, making him uneasy. Then, without a word, the man thrust the glasses toward him. Not only was Carson's handshaking, but his entire body twitched in anguish. Jon ignored the glasses. Instead, he listened and watched carefully as his patient described his terror.

"I believe they're demons."

"Demons?" Jon walked over to his desk, picking up his tablet to take notes.

"I made a mistake in letting them know I could see them. That should never be done. I should never have done that. Now they are really after me. They won't leave me alone."

With one quick motion, Carson pushed himself closer to the edge of his seat and gripped the arms. He was so anxious for someone to believe him...someone to help him. He shook even harder, and his eyes held a pleading look that pierced Jon's heart.

Speaking in a soothing voice, Jon returned to the chair across from the patient and asked, "Do you see them now?"

Carson put on the glasses and looked around the room. "No, I don't see them now," he replied. His voice sounded relieved, even though he knew it was only a temporary respite.

"When you see them, what do they look like?"

Jon's demeanor helped Carson somewhat. He relaxed his grip on the chair arms and scooted back in his chair.

"Ugly, evil, humanlike, but somewhat transparent. It's like looking at a scene that has a second layer. And their eyes are so horrible, dark, penetrating. They haunt me. I can't sleep at night."

Jon made some notes on his pad. "Do you hear them, too?"

Carson shivered. "Yes, their voices are harsh and gravely, like fingernails grating against a chalkboard."

"I can see how that would be very disturbing," Jon assured him. "Do they talk to you? Address you in any way?"

"No…not directly, but I hear them planning things."

Jon looked up. What his patient said next could indicate if he was a danger to himself or others.

"They influence people to do destructive things."

"You mean like blow up things or hurt people?"

"I don't know about blowing things up, but hurting people, yes."

"In what way?"

"By their actions." When Jon looked puzzled, Carson continued. "You know…for example, encouraging a child to rebel, to defy his parents and do something that could cause terrible harm, physically and or emotionally. By weakening minds, breaking down good people, convincing them it's all right to cheat; on their wives, their business partners, with money. Oh, I've seen them strategize and attack world leaders, corrupting them, convincing them to take the wrong path."

Jon made some additional notes: *Patient is referring to emotional harm rather than physical; still, the possibility is there. Need to keep a watch on that.* He looked up.

"If these glasses create so much tension for you, why do you wear them? Why not get rid of them?"

"Because what I see is *real*, even if it's bad. I can't stop. I wish I could. I can't. I've tried. It's like they…the glasses…they pull me." Still wearing the glasses, Carson's eyes darted around the room as though he was looking for something. His fear and nervousness increased again as if he didn't want to see anything, but he couldn't stop searching. "Don't you want to know what is real?"

"Yes, I suppose I do," Jon said encouragingly. "So, do you know if these destructive things were carried out?"

Frightened, his anguish increasing, Carson pulled the glasses off his face. "Yes! Sometimes I witness them happening, or I hear them talking about the results of their interference."

Jon attempted to sort this out. Clearly, whatever was happening was causing real distress for his patient. It was time to change the direction of the discussion. "Where did you find these glasses?"

"My great, great grandfather was an optometrist. Besides examining people's eyes, he also made their glasses. My father lived in the family home until he passed away a few months ago."

Jon made another note on his pad: *Could some of what is happening simply be due to the loss of Carson's father?*

"I'm the oldest living heir; the old building had to be torn down because of structural issues. When they knocked down the walls, the construction supervisor found this locked metal box hidden among the broken and damaged bricks of the fireplace. The glasses and a note were inside. I thought it was interesting, kind of funny. Not real. Stupid. I saved it, though. Here read it," he said, handing over the note.

Jon opened the frail 100-year-old note and read it aloud:

"If by misfortune you have discovered these glasses, I warn you not to look through them. For they shall allow you and you alone, to witness the demonic influence on mortal man. These creatures remain unaware that you see them unless you speak aloud of their existence in their presence. I warn you, say not a word. They will make your life a living hell. Bury these spectacles of evil, for I found no way to destroy them. And pray that they shall never be found."

Jon laid the note down on his desk without commenting.

"Of course, I thought it was nonsense, but out of curiosity, I put the glasses on, and that's when it started. Since then, it has gotten worse and worse. Now they enter my every thought. I can't get away from them. That note. It warned me, but I..., I was stubborn. I didn't believe it. You have to help me." When Jon still didn't say anything, Carson continued. "It explains a lot. You see, my great, great grandfather went crazy, and now I know why he spent the last fifteen years of his life in a sanitarium."

Jon made another note: *Mental problems in the family, specifically great, great grandfather. Are there others?* "I'm sorry to hear that. Are there any other family members who have been treated for mental illness?"

"No. No! You are missing the point! Don't you understand? It's about them...the demons. What I see and hear. What he heard. That's why he locked and sealed the glasses away behind the fireplace!"

"So these demons know you have the glasses? Do they know you are using them to see and hear them?"

"They didn't look at first, but I didn't pay attention to the warning. I talked about them when I wasn't wearing the glasses. Then they became aware that I could see and hear them, and that I had the glasses."

"So, the glasses protected you from them at first. Is that right?"

"Yes. Now, they keep after me. They won't leave me alone. It's so bad…so bad."

"What do you mean by bad?" Jon asked.

"Things I never thought about. Bad things. They try to make me do horrible things. I can't think of anything else. Like, like they're taking over my mind."

Carson was becoming so manic now that he jumped out of his chair and started pacing around the room. After several frenzied steps, he rushed over to Jon and held out the glasses. His hand shook violently.

"Here, put them on. Maybe you'll see them."

"I'll take your word for it if you don't mind. Now, please, Carson, sit and try to calm down."

"Of course," he said sarcastically. "You wouldn't be able to see them anyway. Only one person at a time. That's what the note said. Nobody. Nobody else has been able to see…. I've tried it." By now, he was almost talking to himself. "Why would you?" He went still. Tears began to trickle down his face, and a look of hopelessness filled his eyes.

Transfixed by Carson's extreme reaction, Jon watched him closely.

"Please," Carson begged. "I'm not crazy! I swear! I am not crazy. This is real!"

Fighting to keep his decorum and professionalism, Jon responded quietly, although he was wary. "I believe you, Carson. You see something through those glasses that terrifies you. I don't need to see it to believe you."

Glancing down at his tablet, Jon made further notes: either psychotic, paranoid, or having some hallucinogenic experience. Whatever it is, he believes he sees demons when he puts on glasses. Drugs?

Carson looked utterly defeated, resigned. Still standing, his fingers opened and closed on the glasses he held to his side.

"Don't put the glasses back on, Carson." Jon stood up and gently laid a hand on the man's shoulder. "Just sit. Relax. I'm going to write you a prescription that should help."

Carson sank back into his chair and nodded his head in agreement. He put his head in his hands and wept.

Jon poured him a glass of cold water from a pitcher on the coffee table. Carson accepted it and gulped down half the glass. Setting it down on a coaster on the coffee table, he sat as still as a statue, as the doctor wrote a few more notes on his tablet, and then pulled out a prescription pad and began writing a prescription.

Seeing what Jon was doing, Carson's face began to change. His expression went dark. "This isn't going to help! Don't you understand? It is not in my mind. We are not safe. You," he said, pointing at Jon and warning him, "are not safe. You think I'm on drugs, don't you? Oh, if only that were the case. It would be so much easier to fix this, but it's not! I can see them and hear them."

As Jon handed him the prescription, he tried to reach out to the patient, pretending to agree, and trying to minimize the pain.

Carson, however, pulled away and jumped up from his chair. His personality changed, and he glared at Jon in anger. "You just don't get it. They are here." He waved his arms around. "In this room, …everywhere. We can't get away from them. There's no escape!"

Carson looked at the prescription, and then at Jon. Wadding up the paper, he threw it to the floor and stormed out of the office and into the lobby, catching Vivian with a mouth full of cheese pastry. She tried to cover her mouth, but her eyes grew large when she saw the wild look on his face. Her eyes darted from the patient to Jon, who had followed him out, and back again.

Distraught and breathing in short gasps, Carson headed for the door and threw it open. In despair, he turned to face Jon. "You don't believe me, so you can't help me. No one can help me."

Carson's face crumpled, and he ran out of the office.

Jon's partner, Dr. Tom Peneles, stood in his doorway and said, "Well, you really helped that guy."

"I've never dealt with this kind of condition before. He sees enemies."

"You mean like Superhero kind of enemies?" Tom asked.

"No, when he puts a certain pair of glasses on, he sees demons. What would you say to a guy who said he sees demonic enemies through a pair of glasses, demons that are invisible to everyone else?"

"I'd tell him to throw the glasses away."

"I did. He said he couldn't because he wanted to see 'real' things, to be aware. He said that the glasses drew him to them."

"Drugs?"

"I don't know," Jon admitted.

"Good luck with that one. Hey, it's Taco Tuesday. Are we on for lunch?"

Jon gave him a weird look. "It's ten o'clock in the morning!"

"I'm just getting my reservation in early. You're so popular."

Jon shook his head and walked over to close the door. He couldn't help peeking outside to see if Carson was still around, but he doubted it. The man was gone. He only hoped he could find a way to help him before it was too late.

Chapter Three

Amber

Jon hurried through the large revolving door of *The Shops of Boston*, a local shopping mall where his daughter loved to spend money. Heading inside, he found Amber on level one, outside a skate shop. As he walked toward her, he could not help thinking about how much she looked like his wife with her long chestnut hair, especially when she smiled, which she was doing now as she listened to a tall, thin skate enthusiast explain a laser flip on his board. As Jon approached, she looked up; the expression in her blue eyes turned to exasperation.

Catching sight of Amber's dad heading toward them, the boy quickly headed back into the shop, calling over his shoulder, "see you later."

Amber was a little surprised, but she disregarded it. This whole guy thing was new to her, and she hadn't figured it out yet. Devon sure was cute, though, and he seemed to like her.

"Sorry I'm late, princess."

"You're *always* late, dad."

"Amber, I am not always late."

"I've been standing here, like forever!"

"You seemed to be fairly well occupied."

"You're spying on me?"

"No, I just happened to see you talking with that boy." He nodded toward the skate shop.

"Great. No wonder he left."

Jon couldn't believe it. He had just arrived, and already they were arguing. "Come on, I took this time off to be with you, so let's have some fun. What do you want to do? Mom says that's one of your favorite stores," he said, nodding towards *Forever 21*. "Want to browse? I'll give you this much to spend."

Jon flashed five fingers, meaning $50.

Amber flashed back ten.

He countered with seven and then changed it to eight.

Amber gave him the thumbs up, and they bumped their thumbs together. She walked away from him, heading into the store. Jon followed until she turned around.

"You're following me."

"I thought we were shopping together."

"Whatever."

Jon found a chair in the corner of the store and sat there reading an email on his phone while he waited for his daughter.

Sometime later, she walked over and pulled a semi-transparent blouse out of her bag to show him.

"I don't think so, Amber."

"Why? This is the cutest thing they have here."

"You're fifteen, not a thirty-year-old streetwalker." As soon as the words were out of his mouth, Jon regretted them, but the damage was done. He watched as Amber returned to the counter and nodded toward her father, her face and neck scarlet with embarrassment. The young clerk, dressed in all black, nodded, and gave her an understanding look.

"Come on, there's nothing else here," she walked past him toward the mall exit.

****

Jon and his daughter walked into the warm, inviting kitchen, part of the great room, connecting the dining room and living room, reflecting Brooke's classy, unique taste of hospitality and warmth.

"I fixed a great meal, and you guys are late. Now the meal is cold," said Brooke, a beautiful woman with long blonde hair that hung four inches past her shoulders. Her eyebrows reflected the frustration she felt at their tardiness.

"Dad was late meeting me," Amber said, clearly laying the blame at her father's feet.

"Did you find anything you liked?"

"Ask him."

Grabbing a plate and filling it with a small amount of food, she walked past her mom on the way upstairs to her bedroom.

Usually, Brooke would have stopped her, insisting she eat with them at the table. However, the tension was as thick as mud between Jon and Amber, and she thought she should give Jon the chance to tell his side of the story first. Brooke turned and glared at him.

"What happened? This was supposed to be a bonding opportunity."

"I said something stupid. I hurt her feelings."

"What?"

"It's not important. I just blew it."

"For crying out loud, Jon, you're a psychiatrist!"

23

"And *you* are her mother! Maybe you should be teaching her some better standards."

"What is *that* supposed to mean?"

"I don't know. It seems like I don't know her anymore. She's like a different kid. I sure don't understand her."

"Well, you need to step up and make an effort to know her and understand her. At least give her what you would give one of your clients. I feel like we're losing her."

"I know. I feel the same way." Jon followed Brooke back into the kitchen, where she pulled the over-cooked chicken out of the oven and spooned limp green beans and some quinoa onto each of their plates.

"Maybe it's just a seasonal thing."

"Seasonal? What is that supposed to mean? Come winter, she'll change?"

Brooke shook her head again and sighed. "This isn't seasonal; she's growing up too fast."

"There is so much outside influence that we can't control. It's not like we're not trying."

"Really?"

Brooke stopped to collect her thoughts and turned to Jon. "I never thought that at fifteen it would get this bad already. Joyce and Brian are a couple of years ahead of us with Michelle, and she's ready to tear her hair out. She said it happened overnight. You know what else she said. She said that one day, Michelle was a princess singing Disney songs, and the next, she was doodling some boy's name on her notebook. It's scary."

"I'm more concerned about the boys."

Brooke waited for him to continue.

"There was some boy at the mall. I think he works there. Anyway, when he spotted me, he took off, back inside the skate store."

"She's too young. I'm not ready for this."

They both sat down at the kitchen table across from one another, their tempers now under control. They realized they had to be united and do something, but they weren't sure what.

"Tom does more counseling with moms than I do. I'll ask him tomorrow and see if he thinks this is normal. Plus, he knows Amber. Maybe he can offer some advice."

"Good idea. I'll have coffee with Joyce and see if there is some way she can prep us for what's to come and give us some encouragement. I need to see some light at the end of this tunnel."

"I'm sorry about being late. A very distressed client this morning backlogged my appointments for the rest of the day. I tried to get there on time."

Brooke looked at Jon, letting her love overcome her anger. "I think maybe we should start making office appointments with Vivian. At least we'll get to see you more often."

"Sorry."

Chapter Four

To the Battle

Jon handed Phil his morning coffee and pastry.

Phil peeked at the pastry and smiled. "Raspberry! You are *delightful* to work with, Jon," he said as he took a bite. His expression was one of pure enjoyment.

"I promise, always raspberry. No cheese." Jon raised his pastry, tucked safely in a small white bakery bag.

"I'm going to have to really start working today."

"That's good, Phil. Work is good. What kind of work will you be doing?"

"Helping a friend."

"Part-time work, huh?"

"Hmm." Phil took a bite of his pastry and chewed before continuing. "Could end up being full-time."

"Well, that's great."

"Are you prepared for today, Jon?"

"I believe I am." He smiled and sipped his coffee.

"That's good."

"To the battle, then."

Phil raised his cup in response.

****

Jon walked into his building, smiling. He just knew this was going to be an easy day. Striding across the waiting room, he walked up to the reception window, still looking back at the front door of the office. He was a few minutes early for his first appointment.

"You know, I would love to know Phil's story."

Vivian ignored his comment and nodded her head toward the only two people in the waiting area, a man and a woman who stood up from the chairs they were occupying.

"Good morning, Dr. Rickner. These detectives are here to see you."

Puzzled, Jon turned and approached them.

"Dr. Rickner, I'm Detective Fred Behnken, and this is my partner, Detective Angie Morehouse," a man in his mid-forties said.

Jon looked at the man, who was six feet tall with a solid build, gunmetal blue eyes, and brown hair with patches of gray just appearing at the temples.

"Nice to meet you, detectives. What can I do for you?" he asked with a slight nod, acknowledging them.

"Do you have a patient by the name of Carson Alexander?"

"Yes, he came to see me for the first time yesterday. Is there a problem?"

The second detective, a woman in her early thirties, 5'5" tall, with an athletic build, amber eyes, and short brown hair, said, "What did he come to see you about?"

"Come on, detectives, you know I can't share that information. Not even with you."

"If someone's life is in danger, you can," Detective Behnken said.

His response puzzled Jon. "As far as I know, no one was in danger. Has that situation changed?"

"Are you aware that Mr. Alexander killed himself last night?" Detective Morehouse asked.

Her words nearly rocked him back on his feet, and his expression changed from concern to shock. "No, I wasn't."

"He left a note for you," she said. She showed him a plastic evidence bag with a handwritten note scrawled on a piece of white printer paper.

Curious, he reached out his hand. "Can I see it?"

She handed him the bag. The enclosed note read:

Dr. Rickner, you and your family are in great danger. I know you believe me, and it is only a matter of time before they find out.

"Do you know what that means or who 'they' are?" Detective Behnken asked.

Jon wrinkled his brow as he thought back to the previous morning. "Not really. I can look at my notes, but..."

"It might help us sort this out if you would allow us to see his file," Behnken said.

"You know I can't do that. Patient-doctor confidentiality and all that," Jon insisted.

"Your patient is dead, doctor," Detective Morehouse gently reminded him.

"It doesn't matter," Jon told her with a negative shake of his head.

"Then, we'll be back with a subpoena to review your files," she told him.

Jon handed the evidence bag back to her. "I'm afraid that won't make any difference. I would still need a member of his family to sign a release. Otherwise, I could be hit with a lawsuit."

"Don't you understand?" Detective Behnken asked him. "That note clearly implies that you and your family are in danger."

"No...I...," he thought back to Carson's frantic ravings. "No, really, there's nothing to worry about."

"Even so, we have to investigate it. If you are in some danger, Carson may have been as well, which means this might not have been a suicide after all. Until we know for certain, we'll have to dig further into this," Behnken said. "We'll be back with that subpoena."

The detectives left, and a troubled Jon wandered into his office and sat down on the chair where Carson had sat the day before. Placing his coffee and Danish on the coffee table, he mentally reviewed everything that had happened yesterday during Carson's visit.

It was just the ravings of a mentally ill man, he told himself. *Nevertheless, he believed that what he thought he saw and heard was real.* Leaning back, Jon felt something hard poke him in the hip. He inched forward and reached behind him. His fingers wrapped around the offending object and bringing it out, he discovered Carson's glasses. He stared at them, wondering, *could it be?* Then hesitatingly, he put them on. Nothing. He walked out of his office and into Tom's.

"You probably heard."

"Vivian. Verbatim."

Removing the glasses, he handed them to Tom. "Here, tell me if you see anything."

Thomas put them on carefully, wiggling his eyebrows. Then he gasped, grabbed his neck, and started waving his arms around as he jumped up and over the coffee table. He rolled once on the carpet, and then jumped up and whirled around to face Jon, who was paralyzed with fear. Thomas laughed at Jon as he took off the glasses.

"You thought I saw something, he laughed again. "Just pulling your chain didn't see a thing. Come on, let's get some lunch."

Used to Tom's shenanigans, Jon grabbed the glasses back from him, but instead of giving him a teasing scowl like he normally would have, he gave him a look of consternation. "A man killed himself over these, Tom. Jeez, have some respect."

Tom's grin faded. "I'm sorry, Jon. You know I didn't mean anything by it, but come on. The guy was seeing and hearing things that weren't there."

"What if I told you, I think I believe him?"

"You're serious?" He scratched his head. "You mean about him seeing demons? Spiritual beings?"

"If these glasses were real, would you want to see that world?"

"Not me, I don't want to go down that scary rabbit hole. In this case, I think ignorance is bliss."

"I'm with you. Leave me alone to live in ignorance." Without thinking, Jon put the glasses in his pocket. "Oh, hey, I want to talk to you about Amber. She's uh, changing."

"Your daughter's fourteen, right?

"Just turned fifteen and she is not acting like…."

"Not like the sweet little girl you brought up."

"Bingo."

"Does she have a boyfriend yet? Not a buddy, a boyfriend."

"Not sure. Saw her talking to some guy at the mall yesterday, but...I don't know. She's constantly texting and on her computer. Claims it's homework, but I don't think so."

"Haha." He playfully slapped Jon on the side of the face. "Buckle up, buddy boy, you're about to ride the Big Daddy Roller Coaster."

****

Later that night, when Jon got home, his wife and daughter were together, fixing dinner.

Amber was making a salad, Brooke mashing potatoes. She motioned to Jon to take the steaks on the counter and grill them on the stove. As the three worked on dinner, Jon spoke animatedly about his day. The two girls listened and watched him talk.

After finishing his tale, he switched subjects. "So, Amber, are we on for Saturday? I checked the weather. Looks perfect for a hike. If we start early, we can make it to the waterfall before noon."

"Oh yeah. I forgot. I kinda made plans. Megan wants me to come over and...uh...help her with this project. I promised I would help. It's due like next week."

"Okay. You could go there in the morning, and we could still hike in the afternoon. We wouldn't make it to the waterfall, but it'll be great."

"Well, I'll think about it, but I don't know. Hiking? I mean, will it take all afternoon?"

Jon looked disappointed. "You don't want to go?

31

"It's not that. It's just…well…"

"If you don't want to spend time with me, Amber, just say so."

"It's not that, dad. I just don't want to go hiking. We did that all the time when I was a kid. None of my friends go hiking with their parents."

"But, you have always loved hiking."

"So, people change. I'm not a kid anymore, but you keep treating me like one."

Brooke gave her daughter a stern look. "Amber!"

"No, no. It's alright. If she's so grown up, then she needs to know what the real world is about."

Brook turned to her husband. "Jon!"

"Yeah, give me some *real world*."

"What this all about, Jon?" Brooke asked.

"That client I told you about the other day? He killed himself."

"The one with the glasses?" Brooke was shocked.

"Yeah."

Stopping and turning to give him her full attention, she said, "That's so sad, Jon. I'm sorry. He didn't even give you a chance to help him. Not really."

"He was so convinced…overwhelmed. He kept insisting I put his glasses on so I could see the *demons* he was seeing."

"Demons? Wow, that's creepy. Did you see any?" Amber's eyes widened in mock concern. "Did you?"

Jon reached down and felt the pocket with the glasses. "No, Amber, I didn't see any demons. Sorry to disappoint y…"

"Come on, you two, stop it."

"Maybe he could see the steaks burning," Amber said, her voice a bit snippy.

Jon turned and flipped over the steaks.

Brooke looked from one to the other in disbelief.

Amber looked up at the ceiling and stuck a lettuce leaf in her mouth. "Come on, dad, he was a psycho."

"Amber, don't use that word."

"Okay, fine. He's cra…" Her phone signaled an incoming text, and she immediately left the room, leaving her parents exasperated.

****

Alone that evening in his dark home office, Jon studied the glasses. They looked normal, old fashioned, but normal. Finally, he pushed them across the desk away from him and pulled a note he had jotted down earlier that day, out of his shirt pocket. Reading it slowly, he looked at the glasses once more.

Turning to his laptop, he googled 'devil and glasses.' No articles came up. He typed just the word, 'devil.' Google revealed 33,000 articles. He only needed to read a couple before he was staring at the glasses again. He slowly reached for them, but then stopped. He wondered if it was possible that the glasses were a portal to another world. Another world that he did not want to know existed. He sat there alone in the dark before slowly picking up the glasses and putting them on. He then turned his head in each direction, hoping he would not see anything. Once again, nothing.

He realized that he had been holding his breath the whole time. He pulled in a sharp breath before removing them and then sent a quick text to Tom. "I want to talk to someone about the glasses and what the patient said he witnessed. Know anyone?"

"Our associate pastor," he texted back. "I think he did his dissertation on something related to angels and demons. Ask him.

Jon continued to sit alone, studying the glasses. Then he felt a warm breath on his neck.

Chapter Five

Dark Council

Two silhouettes, separated by a vast distance, stood in the blackness of a gray walled concrete office. In the background, the sound of crackle and pop accompanied the light the flames licked along the floor and walls. The fire was demonic, eternal, and could burn even without substance. The sound, overwhelming and intense, was deafening. One of the silhouettes, the ominous form of the leader Crump, started to change. It's image growing and expanding to an enormous size. Soon the image enveloped the entire meeting place. The other lone, enraged demon stood in complete darkness.

The mid-management demon, Slipknot, stood in the center of the dark room. His left eye twitching, his face a mask of apprehension. He hated any unexpected meeting. He hated, even more, when his lord and master wanted to see him. It meant trouble. Depending on his master's mood, this could get ugly. But he was proud and determined not to let Crump get the best of him. His head jerked when the sound of the fire roared into life once again. Crump's massive, threatening shadow returned. It enraged him even further as he knew this was yet another way to belittle him.

"Master, you summoned me." Slipknot finally said, attempting to disguise his contempt.

"Do you have anything to report?" As Crump spoke, his shadow changed into the forms of different animals of prey. Each form reflecting the degrees of his mood.

"No, my Lord," Slipknot replied.

"Are you sure?" Crump asked. Now his shadow coiled up like a hooded cobra, its head undulating back and forth.

"Is there something in particular that you have in mind, my Lord?" Slipknot asked. He contained his frustration at the master's over-the-top display of power.

"Have you ever known me to be a fool, Slipknot?" Crump demanded, his serpentine nostrils flaring.

"Never." Realizing the Master was in a fouler mood than usual, Slipknot held back his temper. He knew his ego would only get him in trouble.

"Ah," Crump said, reading the demon's thoughts. "We need to review the basics."

Slipknot wanted to roll his eyes and sigh. *Here we go again.* He dared not.

Crump chose to ignore his subordinate's thoughts. He would drum this lesson into Slipknot essence. "What is our mission?"

The feeling of contempt for his Master increased. Treating him like an idiot was insulting and generated bile in his gut. His words spit out with precision. "To steal human souls from the Creator and take the joy from their existence."

"And how do we do this? What are the Four D's?" Crump asked, deriving great pleasure from reading the lesser creature's treacherous thoughts. This demon was as demented and as evil, as they come. He had great potential, so he must play him well.

Trembling inside at the simplicity of the question, Slipknot responded with veiled scorn. "The four D's, my lord, are Doubt, Distract, and Destroy. And, of course, we must never be Discovered. Our work could then be undone."

Crump decided that a little praise would not hurt. "Well done, Slipknot, you have reached the level of an apprentice." His deriding laughter was like acid.

The subordinate thought it best to remain quiet at the insulting backhanded compliment.

"Now that we've made ourselves clear, do you have anything else to report?"

The younger demon, as deceitful as his master, responded, "No, nothing out of the ordinary."

"The glasses…. Where…are…the glasses?" Crump asked, his impatience growing once more.

Slipknot's eyes widened. He had hoped his underlings could locate them before his lord discovered they had no idea where the glasses were. He wondered if one of his subordinates had told Crump to gain favor and to get Slipknot into trouble. There was always the danger of betrayal by those who worked for you. He began the only defense that came to mind. "They were in possession of a young business…"

The leader's eyes flashed red, and his anger soared, making his voice come out in a deep guttural growl. "I appreciate the gift of contempt and deceit, but don't ever attempt to use it with me. Carson has been with us a day. Who has the glasses now, Slipknot? Who? Buried? Lost? Tossed away? Or has someone else discovered their power?"

Although Crump's anger was evident, the subordinate did not cower. He put on an air of bravado, determined not to show his rising fear. "I don't know."

"And why not?" Crump's voice echoed throughout the cavernous room. Slipknot wracked his brain, shifting from foot to foot. "The location and tracking of the glasses are now assigned to someone else."

The leader leaned in, and the two creatures locked eyes. As Crump attempted to control his anger, Slipknot fought down his rage, pride, and fear.

"That 'someone' serves you. And I deal with *you*!"

I have other things I enjoy more than tracking one pair of glasses: souls to corrupt, lives to ruin, anguish to create. Slipknot forgot that his master could read his thoughts.

Crump's form began to change into that of a stalking tiger, then a vicious vulture. Slipknot knew he had gone too far. If he didn't back off, he would have to suffer. Demons did not die; suffering could last an eternity.

"I will find them," he said with false confidence.

Crump's shadow pulled in its fangs and wings and exposed a side of his face. Slipknot saw Crump's deceiving, venomous smile. "You are one of my best...with the blackest of spirits, which is why I selected you to oversee the glasses."

His words puffed the minor demon's ego up once more. It wasn't often that the master dished out compliments, especially after a fit of anger.

"The glasses are the only portal to our world. Do you understand? There is only *one* pair of glasses that allows a person to see into our world without our knowledge. It is imperative that we always know who has those condemning and abominating glasses. Now, do you understand?"

"To the fullest."

"Report back when you've regained control of the situation." Crump turned his back on the subordinate and ordered, "go."

Slipknot Bowing, Slipknot hid his relief at not being punished. He turned on his heel, then gasped, when again he found himself face-to-face with Crump. "This will not happen again." Slipknot swallowed.

"No, master, never."

Chapter Six

Ordinary Things

Jon sat paralyzed until he heard his wife's voice.

"How late are you going to stay up?"

"I'll be to bed soon," he said without adding that the fright of her breath on his neck and the adrenalin rush that followed might keep him up all night.

"Sweetheart, get some sleep. You've been looking tired."

"I will. I think I'm going to swing by the church in the morning and see one of the pastors."

"About what? Us?"

"No, I want to talk to them about the patient that said he saw demons, Carson Anderson. Kinda freaked me out."

"That makes sense. Maybe someone can throw some light on that." With those words and a tender kiss, she slipped out of his office.

****

Faith Community Church was an attractive, modern building with lots of light that bathed the sanctuary; comfortable theater type seating and walls painted in soft, light colors. A reception area and the staff's small but functional offices were located in one wing. The Senior Pastor's office was at the end of the wing, and through clever design, he had a personal entry right to the platform in the sanctuary. The other staff offices were located on each side of the hall, broken up by a circular garden area in the center, with a staff lounge, kitchen, and bathrooms located there. The music room, conference room, and workrooms were upstairs.

That morning, Jon sat in a brown leather chair in the comfortable office of associate and teaching pastor. Cal Shipley. At 6'1" and on the thin side, his blond hair, brown eyes, chiseled features, and slender mustache made him a handsome man.

"The strangest thing happened to me a couple of days ago, Cal. A man came into my office and told me he saw things through these glasses," Jon said, holding them in his extended hand.

"By things, I take it he wasn't talking about ordinary things."

"Unfortunately, no."

The pastor took them and looked them over. "They certainly seem ordinary to me," he said as he put them on and peered around the room at different angles. "I don't see anything. Did you try them on, Jon? More importantly, did *you* see anything through them?"

"Yes, of course, I tried them on, and no, I did not see anything. I still don't, but he saw demons."

Cal whipped off the glasses, and gingerly placed them on his desk. "Well, that's…odd…unusual? I don't know what to say. Demons? Really?" He paused a moment and focused on Jon. "You're taking this seriously?"

"Yes, very seriously. The guy killed himself that night, right after running out of my office."

"Oh, I am so sorry. I can see why you'd want to follow up on this." He shifted in his chair, leaning back a little further. "Well, I can give you the scripture and what it says about demons. I did study demonology in seminary, but that was long ago." His finger brushed his mustache back and forth once. Then his eyes lit up. "Oh wait. Funny enough, one of my seminary students did their thesis on demonology. I'll email that to you. I can't promise that it's all that great, but the paper was well researched. It would give you the basics."

He pulled his laptop closer, set up an email to Jon, and began typing, occasionally stopping to check a few things. "There, I've also sent you a list of books about the subject. Nevertheless, Jon, I feel that I must warn you. It isn't healthy for Christians to become wrapped up in the study of demons. It takes your focus off Christ and what he has done for us."

"I understand what you're saying, Cal, but I can't leave this alone. I mean, the man *killed* himself. Maybe it's guilt. After all, he came to me for help, and I feel like I owe it to him. Even though I only saw him once, I feel like I let him down badly. Maybe if I had done something differently." He paused before continuing. "He might still be alive."

"Don't go there, Jon, you are just opening yourself up to a weakness that can be exploited. You're a psychiatrist. You have dealt with mental illness and paranoia before. I mean, you didn't see anything through the glasses, and I certainly didn't see anything. It doesn't sound very legit to me, more like it was all in his head."

He closed his laptop and pushed it away from the edge of the desk. "Look. Can I be honest?"

The pastor leaned forward. "Of course, that's why I'm here."

"I'll say it again. I believe it is best that we leave the dark side alone. We need to learn more about God and His qualities – what it is like to reflect on Him…to walk in the light, not the darkness. What good does it do to chase demons?" He smiled condescendingly. "You can't help this guy now. He is in God's hands. Let it go, Jon."

At the end of their meeting, Jon picked up the glasses from the desk and left the pastor's office feeling dissatisfied. He had hoped to find some answers, maybe even a bit of respite, but he had neither. On the one hand, he understood why Cal was trying to steer him away from pursuing evil. It was what he was supposed to do. Still, he felt that this was different. Yes, it could all have been in Carson's head, but without the opportunity to study his patient further and make a determination if the man truly was suffering from a specific mental illness, he could not be certain.

As an afterthought, he put on the glasses and headed downstairs to the first floor. As he started his descent, he heard voices. A chill ran down his spine. If asked, he could not have said why. It was probably just some parishioners or the maintenance people. Still, he could not shake the feeling of dread that filled him. He needed to find out who these people were so that he could convince himself that this feeling of anxiety was ridiculous. As he reached the bottom of the steps, he realized that the voices were coming from the sanctuary, and he headed there.

When he walked into the sanctuary, however, he heard nothing. The dreadful feeling began to leave, and he scolded himself for being anxious about nothing. Disgusted with himself, he was about to turn and leave when the conversation started up again. Anxiety and dread filled him once more. Looking around, he did not see anyone at first, but an unexplainable fear made him keep looking. Then he spotted two rather odd, foreboding looking men all in black, sitting at the back of the sanctuary. Caution warned him to stay out of sight while he moved closer to get a better look and to listen to their conversation.

"We have started on him." The speaker looked human, but not quite. He was tall, extremely muscular, almost to the extreme, with a heavily pitted face, dark circles, black, mean-looking eyes, and dark stubble on his face.

"Does he suspect anything, Fotwhort?" This one also looked human, short and stubby with dark hair, thick eyebrows, and a heavy brow. He sneered as he spoke in a high-pitched voice that grated on Jon's nerves like fingernails on a chalkboard.

As Jon looked at them, he realized that he saw what seemed to be another image layered over them. Concentrating on those images made his heart stop beating, and his breath catch in his throat.

"He doesn't suspect a thing, Slipknot."

"Keep it that way. We started on him a while back through his marriage, actually with his wife. Now she's so unhappy, she makes his life miserable," Slipknot said.

Both speakers laughed.

"What's next?" Fotwhort asked.

"Now, we introduce a new woman into his life. One who is prettier, younger, and more sympathetic. That would be sure to prick his interest."

"Is she one of us?"

"No, she is on the *other* side."

Fotwhort rubbed his hands together. "Better yet. Does she know she is being used by us?"

"She only knows that she is lonely, and he is attractive. She thinks she is *serving*, answering a call from well…Him." Slipknot shuddered. "She started out as a volunteer, but lately she's been finding ways to spend more time with him and make herself indispensable."

Fotwhort's grin was so evil that Jon had to force himself mentally to remain where he was. "Oh, that is bad, bad, bad. We do affairs all the time, but this is going to give us a strong foothold into this church."

"The dark one will be pleased if we can destroy another of the Enemies' leaders. When a leader falls, many fall. Where is he now?"

"In his office. They're together…" Fotwhort chuckled, "…working."

Shaken by hearing their destructive plans, Jon crept back toward the staircase and took off the glasses. He had heard enough. *It's real,* he thought. *Just like Carson said. He wasn't mentally ill, and neither was his great, great grandfather. Somehow, these glasses open you up to a world in another dimension. They allow you to see and hear what humanity was never meant to witness. I have to do something. I have to warn Cal that they have set a trap for him.*

Jon ran up the steps and back to Cal's office, where he barged in to find the pastor counseling a woman fitting the demon's description. He was sitting quite close to her on the couch, not at his desk the way he had when talking to him earlier. They both looked up, surprised at the intrusion. Cal quickly stood up. Was that a guilty look or just Jon's imagination?

"Jon! How about a knock?" Cal let out a fake laugh. "I'm in the middle of a counseling session here. Why don't you come back…?"

Jon did not look at the pastor. Instead, he focused on the woman, Marilyn, whom he knew from church. "I'm so sorry, Marilyn. I apologize, but..." He now turned to the pastor. "Cal, this can't wait. I was in the sanctuary..."

When he did not elaborate, Cal helped Marilyn to her feet. "I'm sorry. Could you give us a few minutes? There's some coffee in the break room. I'll come and get you when we're done."

"Of course, Cal," she said, smiling sweetly. "It's okay. Whatever I can do to help in your ministry..." Grabbing her purse, she started to leave, then stopped at the door of his office and arched her eyebrows at the pastor. Then she left.

Cal turned to Jon. "All right, what is so important?"

"Demons. I heard them. I saw them, Cal, in the Sanctuary. Don't give me that look. I'm telling you. Carson was right! He wasn't delusional."

The expression on the pastor's face was similar to the one an adult might give an over-excited child who thought there was a monster under the bed. "All right, Jon. What did you hear?"

Jon took a deep, shaky breath to calm himself. His voice was deadly serious as he said, "I heard them planning. They are targeting this church." He paused and reflected back on what he had heard, sorting through his words as it dawned on him that Cal was the target they were setting up.

"They are going to use a woman to...to get to..." He paused. "I think, Cal, to get to you. They are going to bring you down and the church with you by tempting you with a woman."

The pastor was flustered, but he hid it well. "What? That's ludicrous. What are you saying? Are you telling me that some demon told you that I was going to get involved with another woman, after eighteen years of marriage? And that they would, and I quote, 'take me down and the church,' too?"

"Yes, I'm afraid that is exactly what I heard," Jon replied quietly.

"And you heard this because you put on the glasses?"

"Yes, and I saw them, Cal. I heard, and I saw them."

Cal shook his head sadly. "Look, Jon, I think this discussion, this...fantasy of yours has played itself out. I have always respected you as a Christian psychiatrist, but this attack on me by you. Is it because I wou...could not help you? Well, I'm sorry, but it just doesn't fly." He calmed down a little. "And frankly, I am personally offended that you would even think that I could cheat on my wife. You've known Kristen and me for years." He paused and walked toward Jon, putting an arm around his shoulders.

"This demon obsession you have must be dealt with. Get help, Jon. Find another Christian psychiatrist you can trust. I won't say anything if you don't. Let's deal with this quietly. Keep it between us."

Cal's words shook Jon as he realized that the pastor's response screamed 'guilty.' He nodded his head and left the office, gently closing the door behind him. He passed Marilyn, who was carrying two cups of coffee in the hall.

"I hope the pastor was able to help you, Jon."

Jon smiled sadly and watched her walk past. As he left the church, the knowledge of how Carson had felt, especially when no one would believe him hit him hard. *It's like babes being led to the slaughter,* he thought. *I was right, and Cal knew it, but he doesn't understand how I know. I think he knows what is happening to him, but refuses to believe*

it. Or he just doesn't want to.

Chapter Seven

Research

Jon entered the church wearing the glasses. He looked around; no one he could see and nothing he could hear. He went upstairs to the offices and looked there. Pastor Cal's office was empty. Still he looked inside and in the other rooms. When he reached the head pastor's office, he waved. "Just seeing if Cal is in," he told him.

"No, I believe he's out on a call. Do you want to leave a message?"

"No, that's okay. It's not important."

As Jon left the church, he couldn't help wondering if the reason he saw and heard nothing was because Cal was out.

****

Determined to find a resource that might provide some information about what was happening, Jon looked up the name of a Christian bookstore. His only afternoon appointment that day had cancelled, so he headed there after lunch. The *Turning Point Christian Bookstore* had a country cottage feel. As he opened the door, a small bell tinkled above his head, and the warm, inviting atmosphere made him feel welcome and confident that he would find what he needed inside.

Floor to ceiling shelves, filled with both new and used books, lined the walls and occupied the center of the store. Toward the rear was a cozy area with a grey stone tiled fireplace, a grey loveseat, three overstuffed small-flowered Wedgewood blue chairs-and a slate topped coffee table. A picture of a beautiful deep blue lake surrounded by tall, majestic purple mountains hung over the crackling fireplace. The cash register, in front, sat on a long glass case filled with religious symbols, medals, rosaries, necklaces, and other items. On the wall hung framed Christian sayings and crucifixes, all of which were for sale.

Jon scanned the shelves in the front, and then he headed toward the back and looked at some more. As he did, the bookstore owner and bestselling author, Paul Haas, approached him. Jon turned from the shelves to discover a man wearing dark glasses, his hand resting on a white cane, standing next to him.

"Can I help you find something?" the man asked, with a winsome smile, "I'm Paul, I work here."

"Yes, I hope so. I am looking for a good book on spiritual warfare. Do you have anything like that here?"

"Any particular side?"

"The bad guys," Jon nervously replied.

"Hmm, sounds like you want something on perhaps demonology and how the denizens of the netherworld operate. Am I correct?"

Jon's eyes lit up with hope. "Yes. That's exactly what I am looking for."

As the man turned toward one of the shelves, Jon observed him with curiosity. The bookstore owner stood just over 5'8" with a slight, but healthy build. His dark hair was full and tousled, although he'd combed it carefully that morning. Jon would learn later that he had lost his sight just shy of forty, due to diabetic retinopathy. His glasses hid his soulful brown eyes, and he only wore them in public to make people comfortable. There was no light for Paul these past few years, only darkness.

Paul steered him over to the right section. He obviously knew the store so well that he could move around with ease, even though he was blind. Reaching out, he touched the edges of the shelves, which upon closer examination, Jon saw had small labels in Braille. Finding the section, he wanted, Paul pulled down several books with the title both in English and in Braille on the spine. He handed them to him.

"Why don't you have a seat and check these out. Coffee?"

"Thanks," Jon replied as he headed for one of the chairs. "Uh…cream, no sugar."

Taking a seat, he opened several of the books, but he really didn't know where to begin. Starting over, he scanned several titles, flipping through each one briefly. Paul returned with the coffee and sat on the loveseat across from Jon. He placed Jon's cup on the coffee table in front of him, but remained quiet as he sipped from his own mug, which read, *Coffee Opens My Eyes Every Morning.* Jon wondered if the man knew what it said, or if an employee had a strange sense of humor. Either way, he thought it was funny.

Spreading the books out before him on the table, Jon picked up his mug and drank some of the hot brew, while he concentrated on the titles. Finally, he set down the mug and selected one of the books. "This looks like it might be what I want, *The Unseen Enemy.* He scanned the chapter headings. "Yeah, this looks like a good start. Would you recommend it?"

"I would, yes. I just happen to know the author," Paul replied with a smile.

Jon looked up at him, surprised. "You know the author?"

"Very well."

"Can I ask you some questions?"

"Of course."

Before he could say anything more, a man standing in the reading area watching and eavesdropping, rudely inserted himself into the conversation.

"What a bunch of garbage! Marketing ploys to sell books! *Unseen Enemies?* Really? Let me tell you. He pointed to the book and looked Jon straight in the eye. "I have been a Christian all my life and I have yet to see, hear, or know of a demon. Sure, they existed…in Biblical times, but not today. It's a bunch of hogwash to get Christians off the path they should be pursuing. It takes their eyes off Jesus and throws them into some crazy evil fantasy world."

He showed Jon a book he is carrying. "Now here is a good book on apologetics." Turning, he headed toward the front. "That's what you should be reading, not that evil stuff," he called back over his shoulder.

"The finest trick of the devil is to persuade you that he does not exist. The author, C.S. Lewis, said that. I believe he was right on," Paul commented quietly. "How can one believe in God's existence, but not the devil's, since even Jesus had to deal with him?"

"I don't know, but if that guy had experienced what I have in the past 48 hours, he might have a different opinion," Jon told him.

"Really?"

Jon nodded solemnly. "You can't even begin to imagine what happened."

"I'd like to hear about it." Paul said earnestly.

"That's why I'm here." Jon read the book's front cover and author's name before flipping it over to look at the back cover and seeing the author's photo. He looked up at Paul, surprise on his face. "That's your picture. You wrote this book."

"Guilty. You will notice that I was younger and better-looking back then, and I wasn't blind, but that's another story. "I think you have more pressing questions on your mind."

"I have a lot of questions. Who are they? Why are they here and what are they attempting to do?" Jon leaned forward, giving the author his undivided attention.

As Jon and Paul talked, the irritating man at the cash register up front threw several books down on the counter. He stated waving his arms around until one of the employees pointed at Paul. The man looked shocked and shook his head. Other shoppers turned to watch his over demonstrative display of irritation.

Oblivious to the scene, Jon said, "I can't figure out their motivation or why I am suddenly involved."

"You, my friend, have been living on a battlefield. You just didn't know it. I don't know your whole story yet. Just what you've told me so far, but it seems that perhaps God has called you to the front lines."

Jon told him about Carson Anderson, the glasses, and how he had felt so unprepared. Now he felt almost ambushed. "I never signed up for a battle."

"No one ever does, but that doesn't mean we aren't in one. The day you gave your life to Christ, you were called to the battle. Some people go through life ignoring it. Others hear the battle cry and join the fight. Some are specifically chosen to fight."

"Fight? How can I fight? These are spiritual beings – like fallen angels, right? How can I go up against them?"

"People come in here all the time to buy widgets, symbols, and framed inspirational sayings. Very few are looking for Bibles or battle gear. They settle on symbols they think will carry them through life. It's sad. They want an easy journey filled with success, blessings, God's grace, and all the good stuff. The last thing they want is a war. As you said, they didn't sign up for a battle. It appears, Jon, that you have been given a gift to not only see that war, but to become a part of it."

"I don't want this gift, and I don't want these glasses." Jon reached across the table and tried to hand Paul the glasses, forgetting that he was blind. He tried to put them into Paul's hand.

Paul chuckled and waved them off, saying, "they won't help me. You, my friend, have received the gift of actual physical sight to see what only faith allows the rest of us to imagine. Jon, don't say no to this. Don't tell God you can't, or won't."

The emotional struggle going on inside him played across Jon's face. *I can't do this,* he thought. *This needs someone with a lot deeper faith than I have. Doesn't it? Still, no one else can see what I see through these glasses. If I don't do something, Cal and the church could fall. That would affect all the parishioners.*

Feeling a new responsibility, Jon spoke hesitantly, "Okay, so let's say I accept this call to see and participate in this battle. I mean, hypothetically. I can't fight without a weapon. Right? What kind of weapon would I use?"

"You own a Bible?" Paul asked.

"Yes, of course. I try to spend time reading every day…well…many days…"

"There's your weapon, a living sword."

"A leather book?" Jon was incredulous.

"Seriously, I'm not kidding. I've seen these men…demons…whatever, and they are powerful. I doubt that just words…all right, *God's* words…but words? Not much of a weapon."

Paul quoted the Bible, *"For the word of God is living and active and sharper than any two-edged sword, and piercing as far as the division of the soul and spirit, of joints and marrow, and able to judge the thoughts and intentions of the heart."* He stood up, walked over to another section, and chose a book. "It is the only weapon you will need, and the only one that will work against that kind of power." Paul said, adding with his eyebrows raised, "Unless, you have a better idea."

"No, I guess not," Jon admitted.

"Then start using it. And get to know your weapon well - as any good soldier would do." Paul gave him two books: a new leather Bible with in-depth concordance and commentary, and his own book, *Unseen Enemies.*

Jon headed up front to pay for the books. Paul accompanied him and stood behind the cash register.

"No charge. It's on me. If you really are seeing what you say you are, it's the least I can do." He placed a bookmark in both gifts and handed them to Jon. "One more thing, don't live in fear. The Bible in your hand says, 'Draw near to God and the devil will flee.' "

"I can't help it, this is new territory for me, and frightening," Jon admitted.

"I understand, but I speak from experience. You don't want to back away from this. We know who wins the war, Jon. You must trust in God. If He brought you to this place, then He has you covered."

Jon's cell phone beeped, reminding him of his next appointment.

"I could talk to you all day but I have a patient waiting."

"Please, let me know how you are doing. If you need anything or have any questions, here is my cell number, or just stop by anytime, day or night. I live in the apartment above the store." He handed Jon a business card and opened the door saying, "But who can stand against God? Not principalities or powers, or things from heaven or hell, not life nor death, nor any other creature."

"Stand firm, and he will flee from you." Paul reached out his hand, and Jon grabbed it for a firm handshake.

"Thanks."

Jon found it hard to leave the bookstore and Paul's encouraging presence, but with the two books under his arm, one a weapon, and Paul's words ringing in his ears, he felt more confident. He knew he had someone he could talk to now; someone who not only believed in the spirit world and what Jon was experiencing, but someone who had some solid Biblical knowledge.

Jon climbed into his car and three the glasses, Bible, and Pauls' book onto the passenger seat. He didn't put on the glasses because he was afraid of what he might see. As he drove off, he glanced into the rearview mirror at the bookstore. *Does my protection lie within the walls of that store?* He wondered. *Or perhaps through Paul?* Somehow, he felt that the blind bookstore owner would become a key player in this war on which he was about to embark. He wasn't sure how, he just felt it in his bones.

Chapter Eight

It Continues

Jon ran up the steps of his office building and into the reception area full of waiting patients. Vivian looked at him with arched eyebrows and then at the clock on the wall. It wasn't like him to keep patients waiting. Strangely, he ignored everyone in the room and leaned over the reception desk.

"Is Tom free?"

"His last patient just left, but he has another one waiting."

Jon walked into Tom's office and found him typing up his notes on his last patient.

Tom looked up from the computer.

"Oh, glad you could make it. Did you see anyone when you came in, like a room full of people? Where have you been? Never mind. You're going to have to deal with Vivian."

"I need your help," Jon responded.

"And so do all those people in the reception area. When I escorted my last patient out, Larry made sure I knew he had been waiting for the last twenty minutes."

"I'm in trouble." Jon continued as though he hadn't heard a word his friend was saying.

Tom looked up from his computer and seeing the desperation and anxiety in Jon's expression, gave him his full attention. "Okay, close the door."

Jon closed the door and walked over to Tom's desk, sinking into one of the chairs in front of it. "I've seen them, Tom, the demons. They're real. I hear them talking, planning, and it's not good."

"You do remember that I looked through them, too, and I didn't see anything!"

Jon sat down across from Tom, on the edge of the chair. "Yeah, I can explain that. According to the note that came with the glasses, only one person at a time can use them and see through them. I'm guessing that while they are in my possession, I am the only one capable of penetrating the barrier between the two realities. Like when Carson had them. No one else could see or hear anything, so no one believed him. Now that I have them, I can see and hear the creatures, but no one else can." He looked at Tom expectantly. "That makes sense, right?"

"This whole thing doesn't make sense. It sounds like some kinda medieval fairytale."

"I know, I know. At first, it sounds crazy, none of it makes any sense, but then it does. Remember when our group did a study on this: the enemy, the invisible enemy of God and us, Satan and his demons? Nothing about this contradicts what we studied. It's just that now…it's personal. It's like I've been given an opportunity to see and experience it, not that I want it, because I don't, but now that the door has opened to me, I can't ignore it."

Tom looked at him just like he was one of his other mentally ill patients.

Jon knew that look, and it frustrated him. *Now I know how Carson felt when he ran out of here screaming,* he thought. "Tom, you're my best friend. You know I am not crazy. If you don't believe me, who will?"

"Alright, I guess I have no reason *not* to. Just because I haven't personally experienced it, doesn't mean it isn't true. Right? That is a solid premise. I believe you. I just wish we had more proof other than just your personal experience and that guy who killed himself."

"Thank God, Tom." The relief in his voice was sincere, as he stood up. "I really need you to back me up. Thanks."

Feeling like he had another ally, in addition to Paul, Jon walked back to the lobby and motioned for his next patient to join him. "I'm sorry, Larry, I had a personal situation this morning. I hope I didn't inconvenience you too much."

Jon followed Larry into his office. It was a long day and by the end of it, Jon looked at his watch and raced home.

Chapter Nine

Books

As he pulled into his driveway at home, Jon glanced at the clock and realized that for once, he was on time. He walked inside and set the Bible and the book on the kitchen counter.

"Hey, perfect timing. I want to leave a little early for Bible Study. I'm bringing the lasagna, and it needs to be reheated when we get there," Brooke said as she walked over to see what he had purchased. "You bought a Bible?" she asked him.

"This morning I ran by that new Christian bookstore, *The Turning Point*, on Barnett and picked up a couple of things."

"I didn't know there was a store on Barnett."

"It's in the old Miller Building. The owner fixed it up; did a good job. It is very comfortable and inviting. Nice man, too."

"I'm glad you finally got your own Bible instead of reading off mine on Sunday mornings."

"Where's Amber?"

"She ate a little while ago. Said she had a ton of homework and went back upstairs. I think she's ensconced for the night."

As they left the house, Jon slipped on the glasses and looked back inside. So far so good, he saw nothing unusual. Pulling the door shut and locking it, he turned around and came face-to-face with his wife.

"When did you start wearing glasses?"

"Today."

"What made you think you needed glasses?"

"I felt I wasn't seeing things very clearly."

"They're kind of odd looking. Do they help?"

"Not really," Jon admitted.

A look of concern crossed her face. "Is there anything you aren't telling me?"

"Just a wild day of discovery."

"You are one very interesting man," she said before kissing him on the cheek.

Jon was surprised and pleased. "Thank you," he said, sliding the glasses off and putting them back in his shirt pocket. Then placing his arm around his wife, he walked her to the car.

****

Five couples and two single people sat in a large living room, Bibles and the latest Christian book they were reading in their laps. Decorated in burgundy and beige with accents of deep brown, the room was warm and inviting – the perfect setting for a home Bible Study. Most of the group had been meeting for six years and were friends as well as members of the same church. Jon was usually a good contributor to the meetings, but his mind was so preoccupied with the new world that had opened up to him that he found it difficult to concentrate.

Nathaniel, the group leader said, "I hope most of you have met Carol and George. They are new to the church and want to get involved in a Connect Group, so they are trying us out this week. Welcome! Hope we don't scare you away."

The group welcomed them by calling out, "Hi," and "Glad you're here."

"We're using our secret weapon tonight, Brooke's lasagna," one of the group members said. "That should bring you back."

The group laughed.

Nathaniel continued. "Okay, we're on week three of *Marriage, Money & Mayhem*. Let's start with…."

"Hey Nat, before we get going, can I share something important," Jon asked.

"Of course, which is it, the marriage, the money, or the mayhem?"

"This is probably going to sound really strange."

"Nothing new there," one of the men chimed in.

"Nevertheless, give me a chance to get through what I'm going to tell you." Jon looked around the room as everyone gave him their attention. "A few days ago, I had a client come into my office and told me that he could see spiritual beings…demons through a specific pair of glasses - these glasses, in fact." Jon held up the glasses. "I didn't believe him. He was in distress, overwhelmed."

Jon looked around as one person was on their cell phone texting, another was leafing through their Bible. The others looked at him curiously.

"This patient was so upset by what he said he saw and what he heard that he ran out of my office. That night he killed himself."

"That's terrible. I'm sorry, Jon," one of the wives said.

The group murmured their sympathy and listened more closely. Jon grew a bit nervous and he looked at Brooke, who frowned at him. Expecting Tom to back him up, he was surprised to see his friend give him a little 'no' shake of the head.

"Let me cut to the chase. The next day I found the glasses and later, I put them on at the church. What I saw…well, let me say I heard them first. I heard voices and followed them to the Sanctuary."

The new couple looked at each other before turning to stare at Jon. Alan squinted his eyes and leaned forward. The others reacted with curiosity but skepticism.

Nathaniel intervened. "Uh Jon, maybe we should cover this topic after we are done with our study."

"Nat, this is really important. Don't cut me off, man. I must tell you guys what I discovered. I went to the Sanctuary, and I saw these…creatures…all black and somewhat odd looking. They looked human-like, but they weren't. There was such an environment, a thick pervasive feeling of evil." He wiped the sweat from his forehead. "They were talking and planning. They had a strategy to…attack our church."

"Jon," Nathaniel said firmly, trying to stop the flow of words, but Jon continued.

"Listen to me. They talked about working on one of the church leaders. I don't want to tell you the details, but they were very specific, and they were laughing and talking about how once they got to this leader, the whole church would fall."

Jon looked around the room as everyone fell silent. "Then they planned exactly how they would set him up. You have to believe me. Because then I saw what they had planned start to happen." Jon paused. He had no more words, and they didn't seem to be buying it. "You know me. I'm not crazy. I have seen it. Seen *them* with my own eyes…with these glasses."

Jon pulled the glasses from his shirt pocket as one of the guys reached out his hand. "Let me see."

Jon handed him the glasses. Alan put them on.

Brooke leaned over to Jon and whispered, "You didn't tell me they were *those* glasses!"

Jon ignored her and watched Alan.

"I don't see anything," Alan said.

"I think they may only work for one person at a time."

"Well, that's kinda convenient," Jackie said teasingly.

Everyone laughed.

Alan looked around the room, shook his head, and removed them. "They just seem like plain glasses."

"Let me try," Chuck, a tall, muscular man said.

Alan handed them to Chuck, who put them on and looked around room.

"I don't see anything either. Is this one of your psychiatrist practical jokes again?"

"Hey, let's get back to our study," Nathaniel interrupted again. "We can all try them on afterwards. We're probably the worst group for sticking to the subject."

"Squirrel!" Tom shouted and the group laughed.

"Why don't you tell us more over dessert, where you'll only have to compete with Gina's brownies and a sugar high," Nathanael said, giving in. He realized that Jon had a mental grip on this subject and like a dog with a chew toy, he wasn't about to let it go.

Jon opened his mouth to say something, but Brooke gave him a small warning shake of her head. She was afraid that if her husband got started, he would not shut up until he embarrassed them both.

The group went back to the book they were studying and for the next twenty minutes, Jon sat wondering why people did not seem to care that they were under attack by an enemy that wanted to destroy them.

The group ended their discussion and headed into the kitchen, chatting about many things and avoiding Jon's topic. Tom came up behind Jon, grabbed him and pulled him into the bathroom.

"What was that all about?"

"Tom, what I heard them planning, and thinking…what they are capable of doing. We have to warn…"

"Whoa, slow down. Let's get more information on this before you bring it to the shark tank," he advised, thinking that at the rate his friend was speeding down this path, he would need to start counseling him, and soon. He knew that Jon wasn't crazy, maybe just a little over zealous. "I'll help you, but remember I didn't see anything."

"I'm not making this up. You believe me, right?"

"I didn't say I didn't believe you. You just have to dig a little deeper before you go all crazy psychiatrist on the group."

"You *said* you believed me in the office."

"I don't know, buddy! You are making it hard! Why should they believe you? What proof do you have? Put on your professional hat. What proof do you have? And if you continue acting like this…like tonight, no one's ever going to believe you."

Feeling betrayed and confused, Jon walked out of the bathroom angry, wearing the glasses once more. Most of the group was standing mostly in the kitchen, getting their food. They met him with silence and quickly looked down at their plates with a sudden interest in the lasagna.

Jon snatched his Bible from the coffee table and walked out the front door. Brooke followed him without a word. Stepping off the porch, he heard a voice and spun around to see two demons outside the front window of the house.

"I don't know what got them all started talking about us, but it ended up rather well, wouldn't you say?" The taller, uglier demon said to the other.

Jon whipped off the glasses. Clutching them tightly in his hand, he opened the car door and sat shaking behind the wheel.

Chapter Ten

Changes

Later that night, Jon sat in his home office reading the book he had received from the bookstore owner. His Bible was also open and he was jotting down notes on his laptop. He was so absorbed that he did not realize Brooke had entered the room.

"Hey Super Guy, do you know what time it is?"

Startled, he looked up at her, then down at the time on his computer. "No, but this is fascinating. I mean listen to this."

"Whoa." She held up a hand. "I'm sure it is spellbinding, but it's late, maybe tomorrow." She walked softly to stand in front of him. "You disappeared after we got home, and Amber wanted to talk to you about something. She even came up here once, but she said you were talking to yourself, and she didn't want to disturb you."

"I didn't even see her," Jon admitted.

"Obviously." Brooke gave him a hopeless look.

She did not understand what was happening to her husband. All she knew was that his patient's death and the mysterious glasses he had left with Jon had done something that had changed him – changed him in a way that made their real life more difficult. She wished that Carson Anderson had never entered their lives. She wished he had gone to some other doctor with his insanity. She almost wished he had died before… No. She could not allow herself to go in that direction. *Why did I think that?* she wondered.

Her obvious irritation made Jon stop and give her his full attention. "Okay Brooke, what do you want me to do?"

"Let's see... Remember that you have a family for starters. Maybe you could help in the kitchen after dinner, or I don't know, open the mail? Be aware that you have a daughter who has been trying to talk to you. Remember that you have a wife who would like to interact with her husband instead of his shadow."

"Come on, Brooke, that's not fair. I am usually good. It's just that this..."

"I know. I know...the glasses. Maybe everything you have hinted at is true. Then again, maybe the glasses have cast a mystical power over you that is taking over your life. Because that's all you seem to think about anymore."

"Really?"

"Yes Jon, really. Those glasses have hijacked your life."

"You don't understand how critical and powerful this is."

Brooke moved closer to the desk and picked up the glasses. Putting them on, she looked around. "Nothing, Jon. I see absolutely nothing! They're just glasses, worthless ones, too, if you ask me. They aren't even prescription. Otherwise, how could everyone see through them without their vision becoming blurry? They're just an old pair of beat-up frames with glass in them."

"I wish that were true."

"Just get rid of them. This is real life, not some medieval horror story that doesn't even affect us. Your obsession is wrecking our lives, and we cannot afford it. Our daughter is going through a difficult time, and she needs us. She needs you."

"Maybe not."

"What!" The shock of his words rocked her back a step.

"Maybe this isn't some medieval horror story, but real and powerful. Maybe this is going to affect all of us." In his gut, he feared that somehow it had already begun.

His words not only surprised her, they planted a seed of fear in her heart, and she decided right then to fight back. "Well, not me! I will not be a party to this nonsense. Keep it out of this house, Jon. Moreover, keep it out of the Bible study group. We are there to study what God wants us to learn, not explore some fantasy realm from the mind of a lunatic. I don't understand why you've become enamored with all this, but you need to drop it."

Her words were like a slap in the face. "This isn't like you, Brooke. You have never reacted to any of my patient's problems or my theories like this." He looked at her, undecided how to respond. "But maybe you're right."

She sighed in resignation and fatigue. There was no point in arguing any more that night. "Whatever, just come to bed. It's after one o'clock."

"I will. I just need to finish this. I'm in the middle of an important section. I won't be long. Five minutes, tops."

Her anger flared up again, and Brooke stormed out of the room in frustration. Jon forgot her almost immediately as he bent back over the book and continued typing on his laptop.

His wife returned a few moments later, gave the study door an exaggerated punch, and threw a blanket and pillow into the middle of the room. "I hope you and your invisible friends enjoy spending the night together."

Jon looked up startled but said nothing. He didn't know what to say that would change her feelings or calm her down. *What have I gotten myself into?* He thought miserably. He never dreamed that the battle would drive a wedge between him and those he loved, especially Brooke.

Picking up the glasses, he put them on. He was about to remove them when he heard voices. Panic shot through him and his heart began beating rapidly. Quickly, he looked around but saw nothing. Then realizing that the voices were coming from down the hall, he stood up and headed for his daughter's room. He pushed open the door.

"Dad!" His sudden intrusion had frightened her, so her voice was almost a screech.

"What are you doing up this late? And on your computer?"

"I'm…uh…talking to a friend. Friends. We have an…a…an assignment that we're doing together. It's complicated."

"Well, tell your friends goodnight," Jon said calmly but firmly, relieved that the voices did not belong to demons. "Turn off your computer and go to bed. You can finish this tomorrow."

Anger filled Amber's voice. "This is important. Tomorrow just won't…."

"Amber," Jon said cutting her off sternly.

"Fine! I will!"

"Now, Amber." He paused. "Right now."

She slammed her laptop shut, and as Jon closed her door, he heard her say under her breath, "you are so clueless."

Brooke stood outside the door of their bedroom. She had listened to the exchange between Jon and their daughter. While Jon was concerned, and trying, and Amber was lying, she felt that he had handled the situation all wrong. It just added another notch on her gun and made her even angrier. When he came out of Amber's room, Brooke, fuming, with her arms crossed, ambushed him in the hallway.

"Maybe you should've let her explain further. It's as though you suddenly know all the answers. No one can color outside of your box – your new, strange box! You're doing everything you can to push everyone away, especially Amber and me."

Turning, she stomped into their bedroom and slammed the door.

Chapter Eleven

The Devil in the Church

At the stroke of midnight, a choking, almost caustic gloom permeated the inside of the sanctuary of the Faith Community Church, making it feel more like a place of doom instead of peace. If a passerby had happened to look through the windows, they might have glanced once and turned to leave. Yet something would have made them turn back with an uneasy feeling that there was movement inside. A not normal movement like that of a pastor walking, but the movement of dark transparent shadows whose very presence would instill uncontrollable shivering to anyone unfortunate enough to witness it.

Inside the sanctuary, the shapes were indistinct, slowly forming into humanlike, but ugly creatures with distorted fearsome features. The room began to fill. Some seemed to materialize out of thin air. Others appeared to come up through the floor, dark and wispy with frightening shapes that pulsed with animosity and hate as they coalesced into solid beings of form.

A few sat while others stood around conversing in low voices. Their hate warred with the love and compassion that normally filled the large room. The battle was so tangible that the atmosphere felt electrified by the conflict. None of the summoned participants wanted to be there. A meeting of this sort tended to turn nasty, thanks to the caustic nature of their leader.

"So, why are we here?" One of the demons asked those standing around him.

Slipknot gave him a look of disgust. He was not thrilled about being there either, but it was sure better than being summoned for a one-on-one meeting. At least, he hoped that was the case. "What do you care? We've been called, so we come."

"I don't like it either," a third demon growled. "I was right in the middle of an intense argument between two people in a bar. A fight broke out, and someone pulled out a gun. I was just getting more involved when the call came." He made an ugly face of evil delight as he thought about the scene he had left with fists, chairs, glasses of beer, and bodies flying. "I could have made it so much worse."

"That's too bad," the first demon said with a wicked grin. "Nothing like a good fight."

"Well, I'm glad we got the call," Fotwhort said. "It means something's up. We haven't met like this since before the last rash of tornadoes. Maybe there's something in the wind." He snickered at his own pun as did the others of his group except for the third demon.

Crump, the leader of this group, finally appeared, making a grand and frightening entrance that startled the other demons. His temperament was blacker and fouler than it had been during his previous meeting with Slipknot. Fortunately, he kept the fire burning in the depth of his eyes instead of the surroundings as he had in his office. The demons stopped their chatter and turned their attention to him with anticipation. Hoping this meeting would bring on some new disaster on the humans, those reprehensible creatures that the Creator loved and protected.

Crump's gravelly voice was so deep and gruff that no one dared disobey him. Although their hatred and arrogance helped them put up a brave front, none of them wanted to suffer the consequence of his anger should he be provoked.

"All right, Cherubs, shut up, and listen."

Although humans thought of cherubs as cute little babies with small fluttery wings, cherubs were actually manlike in appearance with double-wings and were the guardians of God's glory. The demons got a good laugh over this misnomer and, as such, often used it as a slam against each other.

"I've called you here because we are in a critical situation! You are in a critical situation, and I am not going to take heat for your incompetence."

The demons exchanged glances, each one shooting accusing glares at the others.

"Your reports, every one of them," he said, making a point to look at each demon in the eye, "are incomplete and show a lack of ingenuity and commitment. Moreover, I have had it, and I am not putting up with it any longer! From now on, we're stepping it up...."

Arrogant as ever, Slipknot interrupted him. "What are you talking about? I've been...."

"Shut up!" Tongues of flame-filled his eyes, making them a fiery red. "I didn't ask for your opinion. And you!" He pointed to the third demon. "That last incident with the lawyer – weak, pitiful, and no follow-through. What kind of demon are you? I know some mean-spirited humans who could do a better job than you without any influence on our part. You had better turn that around. And this report," he indicated a floating video screen with a photo and writing. "What were you thinking? Incompetent idiot!" With one

73

swift movement, he smashed his scaly open hand against the creature's large head. Launching him across the room, his curses filling the already foul air. "That's more like it - a little show of emotion and evil. I want to see and hear more of it, lots of it!"

Shaking, he turned to another demon. "And you, Fotwhort, you are the most disappointing of them all. *You alone, all by yourself,* have jeopardized the entire regiment, no, the whole army with your lack of skill and inability. It's disgusting and inexcusable. Your laziness will no longer be tolerated."

The lead demon stalked over to Slipknot in the front row of seats and grabbed him by the neck, pulling him to his feet. The arrogant demon resisted, but Crump had him in his grip. With one mighty hand, he lifted Slipknot up off the floor as high as his arm would extend and shook him. "I thought we had settled this issue in our last meeting."

"Arrgggkkkk!" Slipknot tried to speak, but no words could slip past the choking sounds he made.

Shaking him like a dog, Crump finally threw him roughly to the sanctuary floor.

"One assignment, that's all you had. One assignment! Keep track of the glasses! Is that too much to expect? Apparently so."

The demons stared at each other, exchanging sneering glances.

Crump looked around the room and pointing accusingly at Slipknot with a gnarled finger, "I want you all to know that if the Master decides to punish us, it will be because of him,"

The other demons reacted with outrage and turned on Slipknot threateningly. As much as they feared the leader's rage, it was nothing compared to what the Master could do to them for their incompetence. He wasn't the Dark Lord for nothing. No one wanted to experience hell's full fury. The agony would be unbearable.

Crump continued, "He's put us all in danger of the Master's wrath because of his overwhelming incompetence." Reaching down, Crump dragged Slipknot to his feet and shook him again. Releasing him, he spat in his face. Then he turned his rage onto one of the lesser demons.

"Now. You," he pointed to Fotwhort, "and you, and you, and you!" The viciously enraged leader began pointing around the room and calling out different demons. "You, all of you, find out who has those glasses. I don't care what you must do, where you have to go, or who you have to destroy, the more, the better. Find the glasses and find them fast. That's all. Find them! Or I promise all of you, you will stand before the Master, yourselves, and when he is finished with you, you will wish you had been born an angel!"

Chapter Twelve

Doctor's Advocate

As Jon waited in line to get his coffee, he looked around *The Empty Cup*. Across the room, he spotted a couple he had seen there before. The man wore a wedding ring. The woman did not, and he knew from a previous conversation with them that they were not married to each other. They were colleagues at work. He sensed more was going on than work.

Reaching into his pocket, Jon put on the glasses and was shocked to see a demon whispering in the man's ear. The grin on the demon was hideous. Jon knew that if the man could see it, he would freak out. Jon watched the man's hand slid a hotel key over to her. She cupped her hand over it and slipped it into her purse.

Jon turned away and stepped closer to the counter, where he got a good look at the Barista. The young woman seemed okay, but he could tell by her expression that all was not as it should be. When he moved even closer, he noticed that she had some bruising around her wrist and arm. Then Jon heard the unmistakable voice of a demon. He saw one flashing into existence on the side of her.

The contemptuous creature began whispering in her ear. *"You need to stay with your boyfriend. He's the nicest guy you'll ever meet. Besides, you can't afford to leave. He'll never do it again; he lost his temper just this one time. It's your fault anyway. You knew he was upset about something else, and you kept talking."*

The young girl looked down as the demon continued.

"And you don't need to tell anyone. This is between you and him. No one would believe you anyway. Besides, with your love, he'll change."

76

Jon watched an expression on her face. She was buying it. *No, don't listen,* he thought. Jon looked around the room; it was overwhelmed by demonic influence on these people. It was an ordinary coffee shop with a non-ordinary influence. Were all the other days he had come without the glasses like this?

"Excuse me," the man at the counter said, breaking into the barista's thoughts.

"I'm sorry, sir, did you say you wanted that with almond milk?"

"No, skim milk," the man replied.

"Got it. Be ready in a minute."

Jon watched the girl foam the hot milk. He knew the struggle that was going on inside her heart and feeling helpless to aid her. *What could he do?*

"Here you go," she smiled and handed the steaming cup to the customer.

Jon paid for his coffee and sat down at the counter, swiveling around to take it all in. Out of the ten-people drinking coffee, three had demons influencing them.

The young barista, Sylvia, walked over to Jon and handed him his receipt, which Jon had forgotten to take. He pointed at the bottom. "You hit another goal, Jon, next coffee is free." Sylvia looked around at the shop, "A lot going on here today."

"You have no idea." Jon took the receipt. "Thanks."

"You bet. To the battle, Jon."

"To the battle," Jon raised his cup, perplexed at the barista's use of Jon's signature phrase.

****

Jon's final appointment that day lasted until 4:00. Disturbed by the day, he decided to stop by the bookstore and talk to Paul. As he walked through the door, the little bell tinkled to announce his presence. Jon looked for the owner, spotting him in the back of the store. "Hey, Paul," he called out as he walked back to him.

Paul stuck out his hand, and they shook. "Good to hear your voice, Jon. How goes the battle?"

Jon chuckled at a familiar phrase. "You know, I say that all the time. I had no real idea what I was talking about, but now..."

"What's been going on?"

Jon took him by the arm and led him to the seating area. "I need to know more."

"Why?" Paul asked as they settled into the chairs.

"Why do I need to know more? So, I can fight better." Jon told him about what he had seen earlier that day. "I'm not at all prepared for this. I've been reading the Bible, getting most of the references from your book. Nevertheless, it's just information all up here." He tapped his head. "Can I face this enemy? I have to be honest with you. I don't know if I have the courage."

"Courage in yourself or courage through God?"

"That's a tough question. I want to have courage through God. But how?"

"First, it's not your battle. It's God's battle."

"But I'm in it. That's what's frightening."

"Yes, you are, but God's given you the weapon and armor. He's also leading the battle." "Look what it says here in his Word." Paul opened his worn Bible. "It says here that *He* goes before us."

The two continued to talk for an hour, Jon hanging onto every word.

"What we need to do right now is pray. Let's ask God to go before you and with you, and to summon his other warriors for the battle to come. We can kneel right here. I do it all the time."

The two men knelt in front of the two chairs, and Paul prayed. "Almighty God in heaven, send your angels to help Jon in this fight against the darkness. Instill within him the courage and fortitude to go and do battle against the evil one and his army. Help Jon to know, and never forget, that You are with him always."

"Thanks, Paul."

They stood up. Jon, his courage bolstered and his fear removed, turned to Paul. "If I'm right, they'll be meeting tonight, and I should go and hear what they're plotting."

"I'd like to go with you."

"Would you? But you can't see, and I don't know if you'll be able to hear them. It seems the glasses only work for me right now."

"There are other ways to see without using your eyes. Besides, two witnesses are better than one. You can tell me what they're saying, and I can always pray while you watch and listen. Why don't you pick me up? I don't have a car," he said with a laugh.

Jon let out a small laugh, too. "Okay, I'll pick you up at 6:45, and Paul, thank you. You have no idea how much it means to have you go with me."

****

Tom sat in a movie theater with his date, enjoying the movie. He was about to slip his arm around her shoulders when he felt his cell phone vibrate. He pulled it out, and recognizing the number, answered in a whisper. "I'm at the movies. Yeah? What? Wait. What?"

People started shushing him.

"Turn off your phone, you idiot," someone called out.

"I can't. I'm a doctor!" He yelled back. Then whispering, he said, "Hold on, Jon." He turned to his date. "Christie, I'm sorry. I must take this. Be right back."

Everyone in the theater screamed at something in the movie, startling Tom. He jumped, and then worked his way to the aisle, juggling phone and popcorn. "Sorry. He turned and handed the popcorn to the person whose feet he stepped on. When he finally reached the back of the theater, he stopped to listen. "Now? Yes, I want to. Kind of, but ..." His face reflected an emotional roller coaster. Finally, his expression turned to one of determination. "Yeah, the north parking lot. Okay, man, I'll be there."

A voice yelled from the audience, "Hey, Doc, take it outside." Tom waved, hung up, and then worked his way back to Christie, who was still in her seat. Digging into his pocket for his car keys, he smiled and ducked low, sliding and stumbling over people until he reached her. Handing her the car keys, he whispered, "Sorry, an emergency with Jon. Do you mind taking a cab home?"

"It's okay, Tom. Go do what you have to do. I'll call my friend. She won't mind picking me up."

"You're the best, Christie. Enjoy the rest of the movie. Call you later." Tom started back to the aisle, climbing over the same people. When he reached the person to whom he had given his popcorn, he took it back and left the theater.

****

At 6:42, Jon arrived at the bookstore. He walked through the parking lot to a side entrance that led to the apartment upstairs where Paul lived. After climbing a flight of steps, he knocked on the door and waited.

Nothing.

Puzzled, he knocked again. When there was still no response, he knocked and called out. "Paul, it's me, Jon. I'm here to pick you up."

Still no response.

Jon continued to knock and call out for another minute, only silence answered him. *That's odd,* he thought. *Paul wanted to come with me. He even asked to go. Where could he be?* The apartment seemed to be empty.

Jon went back down the stairs and walked around to the front of the store, thinking he might be there. He tried the knob, but the door was locked, so he knocked. "Paul, are you in there? It's me, Jon."

Once more, silence.

Something must have come up. Something happened to Paul.

Jon was going to have to go to the meeting without him.

Alone.

Chapter Thirteen

The Other Meeting

In the empty church parking lot, Jon sat in his car, looking out a window in the church's sanctuary. The streetlights revealed no one walking in the neighborhood. Tom's car pulled into the parking lot and flashed its headlights. Pulling up beside him and parking, Tom quickly climbed into Jon's car. He looked at his friend and saw Jon's pale face.

"You don't look so good."

"I'm a little off my game," Jon replied.

"What's the big emergency that pulled me away from a great date, which by the way, I haven't been on a date in months."

"Inside the demons are having a meeting."

"You're kidding, right?"

"Wrong, they are in there."

"Then, I'm going back to that movie where the world is falling apart, but I'm safe."

"No, you're going with me to find out what they're up to."

"Here's the truth, Jon. I don't think they're sitting in there, but I do think a beautiful woman is sitting alone watching a movie and wishing I was still with her."

Jon opened his door, got out, and stood by the car, looking back inside at Tom. "Let's go."

"Let's not."

"Are you prayed up?"

"What?"

"Prayed up."

"I'm not prayed up, but I am psyched out."

"Come here."

Tom got out and walked over to Jon, who placed his hand on his friend's head. Tom looked up at Jon's hand.

"What are you doing?"

"I'm going to pray for you."

"With your hand on my head?"

"Yeah, Paul did it for me."

"Paul, the blind bookstore owner?"

"That Paul."

Tom stood motionless as Jon prayed for him. He couldn't remember a time when Jon had prayed for him, let alone prayed for him with his hand on his head.

"Okay, don't say anything. Just follow me in. We're going to slip in a back way."

"Will they see us?"

"I don't think so."

"You don't think so. We could die, and you maybe don't think so?"

Jon darted across the church parking lot, slipping on the glasses. Tom hesitated, and then followed him, watching him look around to see if any demons have spotted them. None did.

They must all be inside, Jon thought.

The two men quietly opened the door to the sanctuary and snuck in behind the back row. It was obvious to Tom that the sanctuary was empty and his friend might be crazy. If only he had known. The front half of the sanctuary was full. Jon pushed Tom to the floor and scrunched down beside him. The thought occurred to Tom that this might be a practical joke, except the sweat on his best friend's face said otherwise.

Through the glasses, Jon was amazed to see a huge meeting of demons, as many as 500 or more in the middle of an argument. He was caught off guard by the magnitude of what was going on, the strategies, anger, and accusations. All the chaos made the hair on his arms stand on end. The meeting was loud and without order, with demons interfering and talking over one another, arguing, cursing, and insulting each other.

Jon looked over the top of the pew and saw a hologram floating in the air next to a demon who was speaking and pointing to the image of the associate pastor, his wife, and Marilyn, the church volunteer. Jon intermittently explained what was happening to Tom.

When he was silent, Tom, seeing some of his friend's reactions, occasionally punched him in the side, wanting to know. *What was going on now?*

"We had a setback a few days ago," a particularly ugly demon said. "He got scared that someone would discover his…."

Jon whispered to Tom, "There is a hologram of Pastor Cal, his wife, and Marilyn."

Tom peeked over the top of the chair in front of him, seeing only an empty church. He was about to turn away when something odd caught his eye. "Where's the hologram?"

The question caught Jon off guard as he was so busy trying to hear everything. "What?"

"The hologram? Where is it? Point to it," Tom insisted.

Jon looked into his friend's eyes and seeing that he was truly interested. He pointed to the suspicious area Tom had seen.

When he saw his friend's reaction, hope grew in his heart, "do you see it?"

"I see…something. I can't make out what it is, but it's blurry and hurts my eyes to look at it." Tom dismissed it. "It's nothing. I probably need to get an eye exam. It's been a while."

"Enough blah, blah, blah," Crump said. "Where are you on your goals?"

"Okay," the demon began. "The wife was angry with him, but now she seems to be more understanding. It was going just as planned. He hated going home. The other woman…uh, Marilyn. She was doing everything to the letter. We even gave her a dream last night where his wife died, he marries her, and they started a big successful church with a TV following. She woke up, assured it was a vision from…you know…Him." The demon laughed so hard he nearly fell over.

"Stop congratulating yourself. What about the pastor? He's the one we have to turn."

"He was spending more time with her. Umm, but in the last few days, he's kind of avoiding her." Suddenly, the demon knew he was in trouble. "I…I…I…don't…."

"Physically! How are you working that side?" Crump demanded.

"Yeah, yeah, oh, he gets real agitated when she's in the room. He feels his heart pounding, and his palms get sweaty." He snickered again.

Crump cut him off impatiently. "Is he rationalizing yet? Making excuses? Are we seeing him turn? He's the target, you fool!" he yelled. "She's just a tool. We're *using* her. He, however, is the *actual* target!"

There was silence, as the demons looked away.

"They've been targeting Pastor Cal. Specifically his marriage," Jon whispered to Tom, "but it doesn't seem to be working as they planned. Marilyn, from church, they've been using her...trying to..."

"To what, Jon?"

Crump was livid. "This is child's play, you fools! What's going on? He falls, the woman falls, his marriage fails, and the church fails. See? We've done this a thousand times, tens of thousands! It's the perfect storm! Get it done!"

The demon hesitated.

"What? Spit it out!"

"Your Lordship, he has been..." He hated to say the word. It nearly burned his lips when he said, "...praying."

"So what? He's their leader. He has to go through the ritual."

"On his knees...out-loud," the demon insisted, trying to get his point across. "Really praying. Believing...confessing even."

" No!" Crump screamed. The screech was so loud and horrendous that it made the other demons shrink back.

Jon's hands flew to his ears, and a look of pain crossed his face.

"What's happening?" Tom whispered urgently. He could tell that whatever Jon was hearing, it had to be bad to cause his friend such pain.

"And…his wife, too," the demon said hesitantly. He paused and nearly whimpered the next two words. "Sometimes, together."

"You idiots!" Crump roared. "You gave him too much time! Picked the wrong bait! You did it all wrong, wrong, wrong! Get out of my site…you are banished. I *do not* accept failure!"

Other demons appeared and dragged him away, screaming.

"It's not my fault," the demon begged. "Our opposers…those who stand against us! I did everything I was supposed to do!"

"Dispense with those other reports. I want to hear about our biggest targets, and what is happening in this area, to this town, and this report better be different than the last."

The demons showed a hologram of Paul, the bookstore owner.

Jon reacted in shock and fear.

"The author! He makes me want to tear my scales off! He has influenced many people, too many. Turned them onto the other side, and destroyed a lot of our work. Report! What is he doing now? How are we shutting him down?" Crump roared.

Discouraged and defensive, Fotwhort said, "it's no good. We've been attacking him for years."

"His history is impressive," Slipknot added. "He seems impervious to everything we do."

"Shut up!" Crump scowled.

"Can't we just take him out?" Slipknot asked, hopefully.

"The Creator won't let us do any more physical harm to him. He's the most vulnerable with his family. How are we using that?" Crump demanded.

"We destroyed his marriage," Slipknot said. "The blindness, the...."

"Don't blather on about the past! What are you doing *now* to destroy him?"

"His son," Fotwhort said. "We've turned his son. He hates his father's religion, scoffs at his faith, barely believes in Him at all. I think that if we keep at it, we might be able to make him an atheist."

"That wouldn't be as easy as you think. Why don't we burn down the bookstore?" Slipknot interrupted.

"It's not the bookstore, idiot!" Crump snarled. "It's *him*! He's the problem. It's what he *knows*."

"It wouldn't hurt, though, slow him down a little?" Slipknot insisted.

"You bunch of whimpering kittens."

His next words sounded just like Slipknot, only mockingly. *"It wouldn't hurt, though*... We have to hit him hard!" he bellowed. "Double up. Come up with something to put a stop to his constant interference, or I swear on our Demonic Father that you will pay! Now you," he said, pointing to Fotwhort. "Tell me more about his son. If he's turned, let's amp it up. A son can do a lot of damage."

"We're working through one of our disciples," Fotwhort reported. "His god is money, and he's making headway with the son. Our plan is simple but brilliant."

"You're dealing with one of their best," the leader said. "This plan has to be foolproof. Take this guy out, I mean out of the war, once and for all. Come back when you have the perfect plan and not before."

Crump looked at the reporting demon, his eyes boring into his. "You saw what happened to the last one who disappointed me, keep that in mind." He turned back to Slipknot. "What's next?"

"The glasses, sir. We still have not been able to locate…"

Every evil thought and curse-filled the black encrusted heart of the demon leader. His mind still throbbed painfully from the meeting he'd just had with the Master. He knew what would happen if the glasses were not found. He had no one to blame for their disappearance except every last demon that stood before him and blamed them he did.

With unchecked anger, he bellowed, filling the Sanctuary with a horrific stench, repeating the vile words he had just heard in the Master's voice. "The glasses are the *only* portal into our world! They *must* be found and dealt with, or else!"

Every demon in the room cowered, crouching low to the ground, shaking uncontrollably, and sniveling in fear. They could almost feel the master's wrath in his words.

Once more, Jon's hands flew to his ears, but this time his fear was so palatable that he, too, dropped to the floor and nearly lost control of his bladder.

Tom was not totally immune, either. He sniffed the air when a horrible stench hit him. "Jon, what's happening? I swear that I can smell rotten…."

"Brimstone." The word barely escaped Jon's lips.

For the first time, Tom felt real fear. Jon's imagination could not create such a smell, but how? He shook his head. *No, it's not possible. Is it?*

"Now go and turn this stinking cursed planet upside down, if need be, but find those glasses and the person who now possesses them!" Crump ordered, his words nearly paralyzing Jon.

From the back of the sanctuary, a church member walked in, right past Jon and Tom. Leaning forward, Jon shook uncontrollably. He didn't see or acknowledge the church member.

Looking around, she spotted the two men. "Hey, Tom, Jon, what are you doing here?"

"Uh…praying. Jon's really concentrating. Kind of…private, you know?"

"Oh sure. I understand." She smiled. "Left my Bible. Can't have my devotions if I leave my Bible in the seat." She retrieved her book and stopped by their row of seats. "Hey," she whispered. "Take care. I hope everything's okay."

The church member walked to the front right past the screaming, angry demons. She held up her Bible to Tom and walked out the side door near the front.

Tom returned his attention to Jon, who still was visibly shaking, and once more started to ask what was going on. Using all his mental strength, Jon regained some control of himself and held up his hand, concentrating on everything the demons were saying.

"Sir, we think there may be some interference from the enemy," Fotwhort whimpered. "I'm not sure, but we've never had this much trouble tracking the possessor before. The last owner…"

"But," Slipknot interrupted, "another has found them."

The leader glared at the two demons. Angry but clever, he realized that he must work with others to be successful and escape the wrath of the Dark Lord.

"What? Who?" Crump demanded.

"We're not sure. We're doing the research now, and we discovered that they are being used intermittently."

"Ah, this just gets better and better and better!" Crump growled frustratedly.

"But, we will find the one with the glasses and destroy him, just like those before him," Slipknot assured him.

"Do *not* disappoint me! Next report!"

Jon's hologram appeared next.

Still shaking, Jon pulled back in surprise and fear.

"We have to keep a closer eye on this guy, the girl's father," Fotwhort said.

Jon reacted with a start and leaned forward again to listen. His shaking stopped, and he gripped his knees with both hands as he focused on his own image. "Tom," he whispered. "It's me. They're talking about me and…and Amber."

Tom looked confused and peered intensely at Jon, watching his emotions. He wasn't sure what was going on, but whatever it was, it was putting his friend through the wringer.

"Something's happened. He was totally ignorant of us until recently. Been a typical church elder, doing good stuff in the community, 'Christian' psychiatrist, basically non-threatening. Lately, however, something's changed."

"He's nosing around," Slipknot added. "Went to his pastor the other day." He laughed nervously. "Talking about us. Like he understands anything." He guffawed. "We couldn't get it all, a lot of interference, but I think we can shut him down. No problem."

"You *think*? No thinking. When you *think* you weaken our plan. Just do it!" Crump ordered. "Stop him in his tracks before he knows too much. Scare him! Use the girl. He is in the same vicinity as the author. Don't let them cross paths, or it will get even worse."

"I'm getting an odd read on him," Fotwhort admitted.

"Who's screwing up on this?" Crump asked. "Get someone competent on this guy. You, you, and you work together. Get results. All right, what's the latest report on the girl? Give me something, anything!"

Jon's image vanished, and Amber's hologram appeared.

"Two words: social media," Slipknot said, rubbing his hands together greedily. "She's falling for that fake friend site, the one we use to lure young girls. She thinks she has this friendship going with a seventeen-year-old skateboarder, who is really a 46-year-old pervert – one of our best disciples. He has used this on so many young girls, and it seems to work like a charm. I don't know how *far* you want me to go..."

"Stop asking stupid questions," Crump said. "Do whatever it takes."

"Amber! They are talking about my Amber!" Jon stood up to leave, but Tom pulled him back.

"Well then, don't you want to find out what they're planning?"

Jon sat back down and peered at the demons."

"Her self-esteem is in the toilet. One of our favorite places. Ha, Ha," Fotwhort chortled. "Parents are bewildered, so many are about their teenagers. They don't know her latest boyfriend dumped her. That was our work, too. One of our teachers has been ragging on her as well, really bullying. I do love working with teachers. When we have them, they can do such incredible work, the damage that lasts for years, a lifetime even."

Crump allowed himself a brief, horrible smile, but said, "Go on. I hope there's more than this."

"Oh yeah, she had a big argument with her old man the other night, while she was talking to our guy. It's the perfect set-up. He's pushing her to meet. She'll be ready if we incite an argument with her mother. She's already mad at her father. Mom is her only ally. So an argument with mom will push her over the edge. It's planned for tonight. She'll run away and meet up with our disciple. He'll grab her then."

Jon jumped up, grabbed Tom, and ran out of the sanctuary. Jon didn't hear what happened next to set the demons off, but chaos erupted in the ranks. As the two men ran, the screaming and accusations escalated.

"Getting interference from another teacher who keeps encouraging her," Fotwhort shouted over the noise.

"It doesn't matter. Follow through on your plan for tonight."

"But there's a lot of praying to go on suddenly," Fotwhort continued. "You know how hard it is to track that..."

Chapter Fourteen

Not Much Time

Jon rushed inside his house with Tom on his heels, his heart so gripped with terror that it felt like something was squeezing it impossibly tight. His mind flashed back through fifteen years of raising his little girl. Through all her ups and downs, bumps and bruises, trials, and tribulations, he had never felt so afraid for her.

Hearing their running footsteps, Brooke came out of kitchen perplexed, drying her hands with a dishtowel, as Jon ran up the stairs to Amber's bedroom.

"Is that you, Jon? What's going on?"

She looked at Tom for answers, but he just shook his head, unwilling to try to explain something that he didn't quite understand himself.

Taking the stairs two at a time, Jon put on the glasses and called out to his wife. "Is Amber in her room?"

"Yes, but what's the big hurry? Why are you running?" Brooke turned to Tom, who remained standing at the bottom of the stairs. "Tom? What are you doing here? I thought you were on a date? What's happening? What does Jon want with Amber?"

"Jon believes Amber is in danger. Someone is stalking her."

Her confusion turned to alarm. "What?"

They both started up the stairs, their steps going faster when they heard Jon crash into Amber's room.

Startled and feeling guilty, Amber let out a little scream.

Jon crossed over to the desk, where she sat with her computer. Looking at her screen, he saw the face of a young man, but a moment later, the face changed to that of an

94

older man with a leering expression, flickering back and forth. The demon standing next to him was controlling the image. Looking wildly around the room, he saw two more demons in the corner across her room.

Amber was frightened. In her mind, her father seemed like a wild, crazy man, not the loving father she had known for all her life. She scrambled out of her chair, knocking it over in her fear and desire to get away from Jon. Running to the other side of her room, she backed up against the far wall, unknowingly right next to the other demons. She stared fearfully across the room at her father.

"Run, hide!" Fotwhort whispered in her ear. "Quick before he hurts you!"

"He has lost his mind," Slipknot said. "He doesn't know what he is doing. Your internet friend will protect you. He's waiting for you. Go to him."

"No, Amber, don't listen to them. It's a lie, a trick to hurt you." He turned again toward the computer, and seeing the flickering image and that of the demon, he picked up the laptop and smashed it to the floor, stomping on the screen.

"Mom! Mommy! Help me!" Amber screamed. She sank toward the floor, wrapping her arms around her middle and rocking back and forth.

Hearing the crash and Amber's calls for help, Brooke and Tom ran to the door of the room, shocked by the scene before them.

Jon stood over the damaged computer, staring at the broken, fragmented screen. The fake young man was still talking, coming through the speaker of the wrecked computer, but it was the demon talking in the man's voice. In the bits and pieces of glass, the image was solely that of the demon's now, it's face whole and complete in each fractured section, even the tiny ones. Only Jon could see and hear him now.

"Amber, are you there, baby? Amber?"

Amber cried and shook, and she started screaming when her father kicked the computer screen again and yelled, "Shut up!"

"What are you doing?" Amber cried, shaking with fear. "I wasn't doing anything. Who are you talking to?"

"That's it," Fotwhort encouraged her. "Lie to him. Make him feel bad for breaking your computer."

"Jon! What on earth is going on? Have you completely lost your mind?" Brooke shouted.

Jon turned to Brooke and Tom. "They're using the computer. They're trying to seduce her!"

Then he turned to his daughter. "Amber, that's not who you think it is."

Amber screamed again and pulled away from her father as he tried to approach her, his hands outstretched in a pleading gesture. He stopped, watching helplessly as she shrank away from him. He turned once more to Brooke and Tom.

"It's really a pervert. The young man is really an older man under the influence of a demon. They're after her. It's a site set up to lure and kidnap young girls. They want to take her...hurt her."

"Jon! Stop!" Brooke demanded.

Amber jumped up and ran to her mother, who wrapped her arms around her and embraced her protectively.

Looking at the screen, Jon still saw the demon face there, only now it stared back at him. The demons in the room were watching intensely, somewhat perplexed.

Jon took off the glasses. "Tom, tell them. Tell them what you saw!"

Brooke looked at Tom.

He spoke hesitantly. "I only know what you told me, Jon. You know I couldn't see or hear…"

Brooke's phone rang, but she ignored it.

"You're insane! Demons kidnapping me?" Amber lifted her tearful face and looked into her mother's eyes. "Mom, he's crazy."

Jon moved toward Amber, reaching out to console her.

"Don't come near me! Don't touch me."

Jon tried to calm himself down. He stands still, looking at Brooke and Amber, he pleaded with them calmly. "I'm not making this up. I saw and heard demons planning to abduct you, Amber, using this sexual predator. He's done it before. He will keep doing it until he is caught and locked away."

Jon looked at Amber with love and concern.

Suddenly, a strong wind blew into the room through the windows, shocking them all. Jon stopped and looked at the glasses in his hands. He frowned. Amber looked terrified.

"They're using that image of a young man on the internet. Do you understand?" He took a step toward Amber, reaching out pleadingly. "They're trying to get to you."

Amber screamed. Pulling herself away from her mother, she fled down the stairs.

"Amber! Amber, it's all right," Brooke called after her.

Jon turned to his wife. "You have to believe me."

"I don't know what to believe, but this does look like…" Her phone rang again, interrupting what she was about to say. She held up her finger to silence Jon. "Hello. Dad! It's not a… What? I don't understand… Okay. Okay. I'm coming. I'll meet you there." She disconnected and turned to Jon, her expression worried. "It's my mother. She collapsed. No heartbeat. Dad called 911. They are on their way to Baptist Hospital. I have to go."

Brooke started downstairs, then paused and turned to look at Jon. "You really scared Amber. Tom, talk some sense into him."

She turned and ran down the stairs. As she did, she saw Amber going outside. The door slammed loudly behind her. She stopped and looked up. "Oh God, please!"

She turned back around toward Jon and Tom, who were both at the top of the stairs. "Go find her, Jon. You need to make this right. I don't know what all that up there was about but stop it. Tom, please go with him. Don't let him be an idiot. I'll call you from the hospital."

Jon put on the glasses and saw a demon in the hallway. He reacted in fear and started to take them off, but then reconsidered as he realized the mistake he made in talking about them without the glasses. He turned toward Tom. "I shouldn't have talked about them without the glasses on. I forgot. They know now."

"What do you mean they know?" Tom asked.

Another demon appeared, and then another. "Now they know I can see them when I wear the glasses. I took them off when I spoke about them, while they were in the room, so now they know. They can't hear or see me now with the glasses on, but they know."

Tom's eyes widened as a thought crossed his mind. "That weird wind that blasted through the window?"

"Yeah. I think so."

"That's creepy."

As other demons arrived, Fotwhort said, "Finally! We have found the glasses. The Dark Lord will be pleased."

"Where?" Slipknot asked, looking around.

"The father has the glasses. He's the one who can see and hear us."

"How do you know?"

"He took them off. I heard him speak of us."

"Don't worry," Slipknot said with a laugh. "He's a fool." He spoke louder. "Do you hear me? You're a fool, Jon Rickner! We can't see you now, so you must be wearing the glasses. Maybe you can hear and see us, but rest assured, you can't change anything! Haha haha! You have no power! You can't save your pastor. You can't even save your daughter. She's ours now! You can't do anything! Fool!"

The demons disappeared.

Jon looked at Tom. "It's a lot worse than creepy. I made a big mistake." Suddenly the impact of all that had occurred hit him, and he remembered that Amber had run off, probably to the very predator he wanted to protect her from. He knew what he had to do. "We have to find Amber before it's too late. They said that she was theirs!"

Chapter Fifteen

The Bookstore

"Look, I know that Brooke wanted me to go with you, but we'll cover more ground if we take separate cars," Tom said. "Drive me back to the church so I can get my car, then we can both look and cover more territory."

Jon nodded. As he sped toward the church, both kept a lookout for Amber. She was nowhere in sight. Tom discussed which areas to cover, and Jon did little more than nod in response. When they arrived at the church parking lot, Tom got out of the car. He had barely slammed the door when his friend took off. Jon drove around the neighborhood looking for his daughter. His mind was almost numb with fear for Amber, the demon's last words reverberating in his head.

You're a fool, Jon Rickner! You can't save your pastor. You can't even save your daughter. She's ours now! She's ours now! She's ours now!

After searching farther than he knew she could have walked, he racked his mind about where to check next. Tom was heading to the mall after his initial search. Jon thought about checking with Amber's friends, but then he realized that he didn't know much about her friends, let alone where they lived or even how to get a hold of them.

You're a fool, Jon Rickner!

Desperate, there was only one person he could think of that might be able to help him - Paul. With any luck, the bookstore owner had returned. When he reached the store, he was grateful to discover it was now open. He glanced at his watch and saw that it was five minutes before closing. When he hurried inside, he hoped the bell above the door would bring Paul. It didn't. He looked around the store. No one was in sight.

"Hello? Paul?" Jon yelled.

Zack, Paul's son, emerged from the back of the store. He smiled as he walked toward what he thought was a potential customer.

"Sorry, my dad isn't here. He left for Chicago where he's speaking at a conference."

"Oh, he never mentioned that. In fact, that's strange because I spoke with him this afternoon. I was supposed to pick him up earlier, but he wasn't here."

"Last second. One of their other speakers got sick."

This news troubled Jon. It felt like too many things were happening to distract anyone who might be able to help him tonight. First, Brooke's mom collapsing, and then a speaker at a conference, taking Paul out of the picture. It was as though the demons were cutting him off from any useful help. At least he had Tom.

"Do you know when he'll be back?"

"Sometime tomorrow afternoon," Zack replied.

"Is there any way I can reach him?" Jon was desperate.

"Sorry, my dad doesn't believe in cell phones, and he didn't tell me where he was staying. I recognize you as one of his regular customers, or should I say counselees."

Jon looked a little sheepish at the younger version of Paul. "I guess I don't buy enough books, huh?"

"You and everyone else."

Zack looked at his watch and then back at Jon. "He's speaking right now. Is there anything I can help you with? A book, maybe?"

"I don't need a book, sorry. I need to talk to your dad."

The expression on Zack's face said it all. "I was afraid you'd say that."

"Why?"

"Because my dad is better at helping people than selling books. He's a great guy and a good counselor, but not so good as a businessman." He paused, sizing Jon up and then spoke. "I have to close the store. That's why I'm here. I can't keep pouring money down a black hole, as they say. And my dad refuses to push books." He motioned to the shelves full of books.

"But, your dad has a great ministry here."

"That's part of the problem. My dad talks too much and sells too little. Too many people are like you. No offense. You spend a lot of time here and never buy a book. We've been in the red for months."

"There are more important things than money." As soon as the words were out of his mouth, Jon regretted them.

The younger man laughed. "It's not your money he's losing. It's mine."

"Touché. That was rude. I apologize."

"You're right about the ministry, but this isn't a ministry. It's a store, and a store must make money to survive. Otherwise, it becomes a leech that will bleed you dry. My dad's a missionary at heart. He was great in the field, especially with mom, but never with the finances. That would have been her specialty. He doesn't have the gift," Zack raised his hands in air quotes, "of business."

"Why did he leave the mission field?"

"My mom died."

"I'm sorry. May I ask how?"

"Drunk driver on a dirt road in the Dominican Republic. My dad left the country, and I left his faith."

"His faith?"

"It was never mine. I was thirteen, but I knew I didn't want a God that killed people."

"That's tragic." Jon paused and thought about the young man standing in front of him. Zack was angry with God. He remembered too well a time when he would have expressed himself the same way. He decided to share what he'd learned. "Unfortunately, another person's free will to drink and drive can have a disastrous effect on others. I don't believe God let your mother die. She died because of another person's poor choices."

"Now you sound like my dad. Maybe we should never have been given free will."

"Maybe, but would you want to live your life that way? With everything laid out before you, no choices to make."

"I guess not," Zack admitted.

"Can I ask you what you do believe in?"

"Sure. I believe in the almighty buck, not the Almighty God. My money has kept this store open more than my dad's God. His faith hasn't helped him much, but he keeps believing. I'll give him that. He continues to 'run the race,' as the Bible says, but he's getting a little weird."

"How's that?"

"Oh, this thing about demons. He believes in demons, like in everyday life. And I'm worried about him."

"He's worried about you because you don't."

"That's interesting," Zack said with a smile.

"Listen, for what it's worth, I'm a psychiatrist, and I don't think your dad is weird or crazy."

"So, you wouldn't check him into a hospital?"

"No, and I have to say, he's kept me out of one," Jon admitted.

"Listen, Jon, right? It's past store hours."

"I'm sorry to keep you."

"No, I was going to say let's sit down and keep talking. Let me lock the door first."

Jon sat in one of the oversized chairs in the center of the store. Zack laughed as he joined him a few moments later.

"Only my dad would take up prime selling space in the store to put chairs here."

"How long has he been here?"

"Five years and $45,000 in losses."

"Wow, that's a lot. I need to buy more books," Jon said with a kind smile.

"You and everyone else. He worked at the mission headquarters for a while after mom died, but he seemed lost. It was like half his soul left with her. He wasn't the same."

"They must have loved each other very much."

"They did, more than anyone I've ever known. When I moved up in my company and started making real money, I bought the store for him. It was good for a while. He finally had the time to write his book. He used to tell me that it felt like the words were burning him up inside, trying to get out. It was important to him to be able to share his thoughts and beliefs with others, to help them see the truth. The past two years have been a business disaster."

"You bought the store? That was kind of you."

"Oh, don't think I don't love him. I do. He's a great dad. I wanted to help, and the bookstore seemed to be right up his alley. Lately, he's been going down this rabbit hole of invisible enemies. I'm scared for him. I'm the oldest and his only son. It's my responsibility to take care of him."

"If it means anything, your dad is onto something. The last couple of weeks, he's helped me navigate some things I never believed in, or even thought were possible."

"Well, I'm happy for you, but that doesn't stop the store from bleeding red."

It became clear to Jon that it would take nothing short of a miracle to make Zack believe what he and Paul knew to be true. Then one of the demon's words from the sanctuary came back to him. *We've turned his son. He hates his father's religion, scoffs at his faith. If we keep at it, we might be able to make him an atheist.*

The two men smiled. Jon was about to say something when his phone rang. Fishing it out of his pocket, he looked at the screen and saw the number.

"Do you mind if I take this? It's my wife."

"Not at all. Would you like some privacy?"

"No, that's okay. Please stay."

Jon put the phone to his ear. "Hey, Brooke."

"Hey, mister. Checking in. It's been non-stop. Mom is having tests done. They think she had a stroke."

"I'm sorry, but at least we know what we're dealing with. When it rains, it pours, huh? Break out the umbrellas."

She smiled at Jon's ability to be cheerful. "I'm going to stay here tonight with mom. How's it going? When did she come home? Did you apologize?"

Jon looked at Zack. He had allowed their conversation to take his mind off finding his daughter.

You're a fool, Jon Rickner!

The look on his face said it all. He should have taken this call in private. "Well, not exactly. I mean, I haven't found her yet, but that's what I'm doing."

There was a long pause as Brooke realized that her assumption of Amber's return home had been incorrect. Her mind had been so occupied by her mother's collapse that she hadn't given her daughter much thought. She tried not to get upset, but to think. "She's not home, Jon? There was no answer. "Okay, don't panic." Her words were more to convince herself than they were for Jon, as he seemed calm, which was good. "Listen, she probably went to Megan's house. Check there. Her address is 976 Anderson Lane. And Jon, don't argue with her. Just bring her home. I can't believe this. We don't need this now. I'll call you again tonight."

"Okay, sweetheart. You're right; she's probably at Megan's. Don't worry. Give mom my love. I'll talk to you later. I love you."

"I love you more, Jon Rickner. I'm praying for you."

Jon hung up and looked at Zack.

"My daughter ran away."

"I'm sorry. How old is she?"

"Fifteen. This may sound crazy, but it has as much to do with demons as with my daughter." He looked at Zack. He knew it sounded idiotic, but it was true. "Three days ago, I would have thought about what you're thinking right now, but a lot has happened."

A look of sympathy crossed Zack's face. "Sorry for telling you that you needed to buy more books."

"That's all right. Your dad's helping me figure this out. The demon influence. It's all so strange, like nothing I've ever experienced."

Zack wasn't sure how to respond. He didn't believe any of the demon stuff, but he felt sorry about Jon's situation. "Listen, if dad calls, I'll tell him to contact you."

"Thanks."

The men stood up at the same time.

Jon spoke first. "I know it doesn't help your bottom line, but your dad and his knowledge of the spirit world has helped me deal with events that are unbelievable. I don't know what I would have done without him."

"I don't understand either, but I'm glad he could help."

As the men walked to the front door, Jon reached out his hand and put it on Zack's shoulder.

"I'm sorry about your mom."

"Yeah, that was a tough one. Thanks, and I'm sorry about the trouble you're having with your daughter. I hope you find her, and she's okay."

"Thanks. Trust me, your dad isn't crazy."

Zack smiled as he unlocked the door and let Jon out. Then he flipped the sign on the door to 'closed.'

Jon climbed into his car and immediately entered Megan's address into his GPS. He prayed, "God, let her be there," and headed east.

Chapter Sixteen

Megan's House

As Jon drove to Megan's house, it was all he could do to keep from speeding. The urgency he felt to find his daughter pushed him hard, but the last thing he needed was to be pulled over for a traffic violation. That would just slow him down and cause more delays. Unfamiliar with the neighborhood, he tried to follow the house numbers, but not every house or mailbox had them displayed. In his frustration and urgency, he passed the house twice before he finally figured out which place was hers.

Pulling up in front of Megan's home, Jon jumped from the car and slammed the door. He ran up the sidewalk and rang the doorbell. As he stood there, thoughts punctuated with fear, worry, and regret raced through his mind. He knew he should have handled the situation with Amber better, be calmer. At this point, he did not know if he was a father looking for his daughter, or a warrior fighting to save her soul.

He pressed the button again, listening to the musical chime of the doorbell as he peered through the crescent window on the door. *What's taking so long,* he thought. *Is Amber inside? Is her friend delaying to help her get away?* The longer it took someone to appear, the more anxious he grew. He stopped pressing the doorbell when he finally saw Megan walking toward the door. Her pace was slow and easy and seemed to go even slower when she saw his face through the window.

Jon felt his body tense up as though preparing for a fight. If Amber's best friend knew something, she might not be willing to tell Jon anything.

At last, Megan opened the door with her usual smile. "Hello, Dr. Jon," she said.

Jon had to bite his tongue to keep from yelling at her. He took a deep, calming breath. "Hey, Megan, is Amber here?"

"No. Is she supposed to be, cause she didn't say anything to me about coming over." She tried to look innocent, but she didn't sound convincing.

Megan's mom, Helen, walked up behind her. "Hi Jon, come on in. What's going on?"

Jon stepped into the entryway. "Brooke and I don't know where Amber is. We're afraid she may have run away. I was hoping to find her here."

"The last time she was over was a couple of days ago." Helen looked at her daughter, her expression concerned. "Do you know where she is, honey?"

"No idea." Yet something in her demeanor said otherwise.

Jon looked at Megan, his eyes pleading for the truth. "Have you heard from her this evening?"

"No. We talked on the bus." Again, the innocent look that did not quite reach her eyes.

"Would you mind checking your phone? Maybe she texted you."

"I don't think so, but sure, I can look." Megan pulled her phone out of her back pocket and scrolled through her messages. "Nope, nothing here." Inside, she was glad that she had deleted all Amber's texts from earlier, in case he insisted on seeing for himself.

Jon noticed her body language and knew there was more to this story than she was saying. "Megan, I think you know more than you're telling me."

"No." She shook her head no before looking up at him and blinking twice. "I don't."

Jon's accusation bothered Megan's mother. Her daughter was a good girl, as was Amber. He was being unreasonable, and this angered her a bit. "If Megan says she doesn't know anything, she doesn't know anything."

"I'm sorry, Helen. I'm worried. I think…actually, I know, Amber is in trouble, serious trouble. If I can't find her in time…"

Helen's demeanor softened. "I'm sorry, Jon. I know how worried you must be. Megan, can you text Amber and tell her that her father needs to talk to her right away."

"Okay." She punched in the words, "Ur dad looking for u. Acting cra-cra. Better call him."

The three stood and waited for a response.

"Why did she run off?" Helen asked.

"We've been a little at odds lately, had an argument earlier. She ran out of the house upset, but I thought she'd come home by now."

Helen smiled. "I wouldn't be too worried. Maybe she just went somewhere to cool off. You know how it is with teenagers."

"I do, but no. There's more to it than that. I have learned some things that make me believe she is in real trouble. She might be with someone who would hurt her. I have to find her." He turned once again to Megan. "Did she say anything about a new boy she's been seeing?"

Stalling, Megan looked down again at her phone as if checking something. "What, boy?"

Her response set off alarm bells in Jon's mind. Now he was certain that she was acting evasive. Being best friends, Amber would have shared everything about a new boyfriend. Reaching into his top pocket, Jon grabbed the glasses, put them on, and looked at her. Standing beside, Megan was a demon whispering in her ear. Jon knew better than to say anything about what he was seeing. They would think he was crazy. And he had to be careful not to alert the demon to his awareness.

"When did you start wearing glasses?" Helen asked.

"Uh, a week ago. Megan, Amber, wouldn't go off somewhere without telling her best friend. Please, if you don't want her to get hurt, you have to tell me."

Jon watched as the demon told her to say nothing, adding that she owed it to Amber to protect her from her father's anger.

Megan began to waiver. Was she doing the right thing by not telling him?

Whatever you do, don't tell him. You will get Amber in so much trouble. She'll hate you then for sure, the demon insisted.

"I told you, I don't know anything!" With those words, she turned and started walking away from him.

Desperate, Jon reached out and grabbed her arm, startling her. Megan turned. Tears of uncertainty in her eyes.

Helen snapped. "Jon, what are you doing? If she says she doesn't know anything, then she doesn't. Don't you dare come into this house and accuse my daughter of lying."

Jon dropped his hand and turned to Helen. "I'm sorry."

"Why are you so upset? This isn't like you," Helen wanted to know.

Megan stood looking back and forth from Jon to her mother. She felt confused as if two opposing forces were tugging at her, each demanding that she listen only to their side.

"Does your wife know you're here?" Helen asked.

Jon nodded. "She sent me." He paused trying to think of the best way to get through to Megan. "Helen, I'm not trying to be a jerk, but I know Megan knows something she's not telling me."

"I think Megan is just upset, as worried for Amber as you are. We'll let you know if we hear anything, but I think you should go."

Deciding to ignore Helen's words, Jon turned and looked at Megan with pleading eyes. "Megan, Amber's in trouble. If I don't find her tonight, we may never see her again. I know she went somewhere with a person she thinks she can trust. But he's not who he says he is. He's bad. Do you understand? This person or people he deals with are going to do something terrible to Amber. Can you live with that - keeping her secret? Anything you know might help me save her."

Fear crept into Megan's face as she looked at her best friend's father. She blurted out, "Amber is at the mall with the boy at the skateboard shop."

Jon heaved a huge sigh of relief. His daughter was still in danger, but now he had at least a chance to save her. "Megan, thank you. I know how hard it was for you to tell me, but believe me, you didn't betray Amber, you helped save her."

Helen stood embarrassed in the hallway. She had defended her daughter against Jon's unreasonableness only to discover that he was right. Megan had been lying the whole time, and that hit her hard. As soon as Jon left, she was going to have a significant talk with her daughter.

My best friend, Megan, thought again, I should have kept my mouth shut and not told Amber's dad where she was. *Amber is going to hate me now. What should I do?* Her mother interrupted her thoughts.

"Megan, I want to talk to you. Now. Come into the kitchen."

Oh no, I'm in for a big lecture from mom. I have to decide what to do quickly. As she walked toward the kitchen, Megan once again pulled out her phone and texted, "Ur dad is headed to mall."

The demon beside her smiled and left. His job, for now, was over.

****

Amber Rickner pulled out her cell phone and looked at the text. *Rats,* she thought, *Megan must have squealed.* She started to text back, but then another text came in, this one from her dad. She ignored it. *Let him worry for a while. Maybe then, he'll realize I'm not a little girl anymore. I can take care of myself.*

"Hey babe, come back here," the skateboard guy called. "I want to show you something."

Amber punched vibrate on her phone, slipped the phone into her jeans pocket, and headed toward the back room of the store. He had never invited her back there before.

Chapter Seventeen

Tied Up

The house was rundown. Chipped and peeling paint that had once been white was grey and black with decades of filth. The yard only added to the dinginess, filled with little more than dirt, rocks, and an occasional scraggly weed. Bits of gravel and hard-packed dust covered the driveway that was filled with a collection of old, beat-up cars set up on concrete blocks. A sizeable wooden porch contained a refrigerator with a missing door, a sagging glider, and an assortment of trash, including empty beer cans and whiskey bottles. The screen door dangled drunkenly from one hinge.

Inside, the house wasn't any better. The rooms were filled with broken and cracked windows that had filthy bedsheets thrown over the rods as curtains. Inside the kitchen, the chipped porcelain sink was full of unwashed dishes, and the linoleum floor was cracked and covered with a myriad of stains.

It was dark. Amber repeatedly blinked, trying to see. She was confused. Dreaming of things shrouded in mystery and frightening images. *What a nightmare. Wait! Why am I dreaming?*

As her mind started to clear, she began putting the pieces together. Everything seemed jumbled. She had to focus. What was going on? The last thing she remembered was walking into the back of the skateboard shop.

Where is Devon? Why am I in the dark?

She was sitting in some kind of chair - like a plastic beach chair. Her hands were fastened to the arms with tape. She couldn't move her legs! They were taped to the chair as well, completely incapacitating her. This wasn't a dream. It was a real live nightmare.

Amber tried to scream. *Devon!* But as she opened her mouth, she realized that a piece of duck tape was plastered across her mouth, preventing her from emitting more than a low muffled sound.

Fear grabbed her heart like a cold dead hand. Her stomach lurched, and she found it difficult to breathe. Where was she? Her eyes searched back and forth through the all-encompassing blackness for any kind of light, and her terror increased. She couldn't move. She couldn't see anything more than a few shapes that were even darker than the air surrounding her. Panicky, her breathing skyrocketed, coming so fast that she began to hyperventilate. It felt like she couldn't get a deep enough breath to satisfy her needs. Was she dying? Was she already dead?

"Oh God, oh Jesus, I'm so scared. Please help me. I don't know what's happening. Please help me. Please!"

Her mind stopped reeling, her breath slowed, and she acknowledged a small seed of calmness. *Don't panic,* she thought. *You're not dead. So try to determine your situation. All right, fact: I am in a dark room, with no light, but I'm not blindfolded. Fact: I seem to be alone. Fact: I am bound to a chair in a reclining position. Fact: I am gagged with duct tape. Fact: I don't remember anything after walking into the back room.* She took a deep breath as the enormity of her situation settled in. *Fact: There's nothing to do but wait and pray.*

She must have slept, because the next thing she knew, she was startled by a faint noise and a light - a sliver of light, apparently from under a door straight in front of her. Someone turned on the light in the next room. She waited, desperately wanting a person to come through that door. Terrified that someone would.

****

Jon's car sped toward the mall, this time with little regard for the speed limit. Traffic, however, stalled his progress. Every light turned red, and as he waited, his anxiety rose a notch higher.

His mind screamed. *Amber! Hold on, baby. Daddy's coming.*

Dark thoughts answered his pleas. *You're too late! They have her already. She's been captured and taken away to await her fate.*

Jon shook his head, violently. *No! No! No! She'll be there. I will find her and save her.*

You're a fool, Jon Rickner! A fool.

An unearthly chill made him shiver. He glanced at the temperature setting in his car. It read 72 degrees. Was it fear? Yes, he did fear for his daughter's safety and well-being, but this was more. This was not the same feeling he had been experiencing since this had all begun. This was something else. Then another deep shiver shook him. Since he was stopped at yet another red light, Jon pulled the glasses out of his shirt pocket and put them on. For a moment, he was afraid to look – afraid of what he might see.

You will never find her. She'll be taken away and will be sold into slavery or made to become a prostitute. She's lost to you, and you will never see her again.

Those last thoughts shook him so badly that he turned his head to the right. And found himself staring into the eyes of a demon with a hideous look of evil glee.

Gotcha!

A new fear shook him to the core. He had been discovered. They knew who he was. He wracked his brain. What should he do? Then it came to him. He began to pray aloud.

"Our Father who art in heaven."

Shut up!

"Hallowed be thy name."

Shut up! Shut up! Shut up!

"Thy kingdom come. Thy *will* be done."

The demon covered its ears and screamed. *No! No! No! Shut up!* It disappeared with a pop.

Jon breathed a sigh of relief. His immediate danger was gone. Now he could concentrate on Amber again. The blast of a car horn brought him back to reality. He stepped on the gas and took off. Although the demon had departed, his sense of urgency still prevailed. He had to get to Amber. Now dread vied with fear. Was the demon telling the truth? Did they already have her? Had they already kidnapped her? Was he too late?

He took off the glasses and drove faster. Time seemed to drag. The distance he had left to travel to the mall seemed endless. Finally, he saw it. Pulling into the parking lot, he drove to the center toward the main entrance. Luck was with him. He found an open parking spot in the first row. Another car was heading for the same spot, coming from the opposite direction too fast. Jon had to do something he normally would never dream of doing. He sped up and pulled into the spot, cutting off the other driver.

The driver was livid. He remained where he was and began shouting obscenities as Jon jumped from his car and ran toward the entrance.

"I'm sorry! I have to find my daughter. She is in danger. I'm sorry!"

The other driver, a man in his twenties, continued to shout until Jon disappeared through the door. Had Jon been wearing the glasses and looked at the driver, he would have seen the same demon that had been next to him, besides to the driver encouraging his rage.

****

Inside the mall, Jon ran toward the Skate Shop on the first level. No one was milling around the exterior, so he ran inside. He saw a mother and her young son examining some of the merchandise, and a young man standing behind the cash register, looking bored. Jon ran up to him.

"Excuse me, young man. Excuse me."

The man turned to look at Jon. "What can I do for you?"

"I'm looking for my daughter. Her name is Amber." Jon fumbled with his cell phone until he brought up a recent picture of her. "This is what she looks like. Have you seen her here tonight?"

The young man looked at the photo and shook his head. "Cute girl, but no. I haven't seen her."

"Are you sure? Look again. I know she was coming here to meet someone, a young man, blond hair, blue eyes, about 5' 10" tall…"

"Hey, sorry, man. I haven't seen either one of them, and I've been here since 3:00."

Jon glanced around the store, frantically. "She has to be here somewhere. Amber? Amber, where are you?"

His shouts caught the attention of the mother and several shoppers outside the store walking past.

"Amber! Please, honey, I'm sorry."

The young man walked around the counter and approached Jon. "Hey, look, man; you can't stand here shouting like that. You're disturbing the customers."

"You don't understand. I have to find my daughter, and I know she's here somewhere. Her girlfriend said she was." He rushed through the store to a door in the back marked *Employees Only* and opened the door.

"Hey!" The young man shouted. "You can't go back there. That's off-limits to the public."

"She could be hiding."

"Not back there, she isn't. I'm going to have to ask you to leave. If your daughter is at the mall, she has to be in some other store."

"She's here. I know she is." He started to walk through the door until he felt himself being grabbed roughly by the arm and pulled back. Turning, he looked into the eyes of the man holding him. Was there a shadow of something unworldly there? He shook himself like a dog. He was seeing demons lurking behind every corner.

"If you don't leave, I'll have to call mall security. In fact, why don't you talk to them? They can help you look for her."

Jon let out the breath he hadn't realized he had been holding. "Good idea. Can you call them for me?"

The young man relaxed his grip and firmly closed the door leading to the back of the store. "If you'll follow me back to the counter, I'll call them."

He paused until he was sure that Jon was coming, and then he walked back behind the counter and picked up the phone. As he dialed an extension and talked into the receiver, Jon pulled out the glasses and put them back on. He saw what he feared. Another demon stood next to the young man whispering in his ear. It was a different one this time, but he had seen it before – at the meeting. It was the demon he had seen on Amber's laptop. It turned and looked right at him and grinned. That was when Jon knew for sure.

They had Amber.

Chapter Eighteen

Alone

The light went out, and Amber realized she had been holding her breath. *No, no, come back. Please, someone. Please.* Amber closed her eyes and took a breath, then forced herself to breathe evenly, slowly. Her mind was clearer now. She told herself to relax, think. *Maybe it's better if they don't come in. Did Devon bring me here? What do they plan to do with me? Ransom! They must want a ransom. I'm so stupid. I can't believe this happened. I should have listened to my dad.*

Her mind jumped to all the scenarios she'd seen on TV. *What if they wanted too much money? Like a million dollars? Stop! That's ridiculous. Mom and Dad aren't that kind of rich. The kidnappers would know that. Right? Okay, enough. Stop thinking about why, and figure out how to get away!*

Focus, Amber. Focus on an escape plan. She tried to move her arms again. *Why did they have to use tape? Why not rope? Everyone gets out of rope. Remember, Amber, this isn't TV. Figure it out. I somehow have to loosen the tape.* She started with her right wrist, secured tightly to the arm of the chair. She pulled and then rocked her arm back and forth, trying to loosen it, back and forth, back and forth. Tired, she stopped. It hadn't budged.

Maybe I can tear at the tape with my teeth. It was hard, leaning to one side and getting her head low enough to grab an edge of the tape with her teeth. It had been wrapped several times with duct tape. She couldn't find the beginning of the tape, so she tried to bite through it, but as much as she pulled and tugged, she couldn't get it to rip. Tired and discouraged, Amber sat back.

Suddenly her hip tingled with a vibration. Her phone! She still had her phone! She had muted it after her dad's last text, but she had the phone! If only she could reach it somehow. In a frustrated panic, she pulled and pulled her arm, trying to tear it free from the restraint until the tingling vibration stopped. Right there in her pocket was help. And she couldn't use it! *Dad! Dad!* She called out to him in her mind. *Find me, dad, find me! I need you.*

A noise, a light under the door, and a voice. Suddenly, the room filled with a blinding light as the door opened. Amber shut her eyes instinctively and then squinted to see who had entered.

It was a small person - a child? No, a short, petite woman slowly moved toward her. Without a word, she stopped and stood there looking down at Amber. The girl's eyes finally adjusted to the brightness, and she could see that the woman held a soft drink. She grunted and pointed her chin toward the bottle, realizing how thirsty she was. The woman set down the drink and carefully untied the gag from Amber's mouth.

"Thank you." Amber's voice came out raspy and strained.

The woman pulled a straw from the pocket of her blouse, stuck it in the bottle, and held it up for Amber to drink. In seconds it was gone.

Her jailor turned and started toward the door.

"No, wait! Don't leave. Please. Tell me, where am I? Who are you?"

The woman switched off the light and quietly shut the door.

"Please, don't leave me in the dark!"

Amber wanted to scream, but fearful she would be gagged again, she bit her lip instead, mentally kicking herself. Why hadn't she looked around? She was so focused on the drink and the woman; she still didn't know where she was.

As her eyes adjusted once more to the darkness, she realized that the strange little woman had left the light on in the room on the other side of the door, allowing a small amount of illumination to squeeze through the crack at the bottom. For the first time, she could make out some of her surroundings.

There was one door, judging from where the thin light that entered the room at about eye level, it must be a few steps up a staircase of maybe five or six steps. That would mean a basement or a split-level. She looked left and realized that there were small windows, painted black, high on the wall. Yes, she was in a basement. A split-level would have larger windows. She concentrated hard trying to distinguish the darker shapes that filled the area, but she couldn't make out anything. Maybe it was furniture or boxes, definitely some bulky things, but totally unrecognizable. Although she wasn't cold, it felt damp and chilly, so it probably was an old house or maybe a small store. Store? Could she be in the basement of the skateboard shop?

She tried once more to pull her arms against the tape, with the same result. Her hip vibrated again. Someone was trying to reach her. *Dad? Daddy?* She wiggled her hips. If people could accidentally butt call, maybe she could butt answer. *Turn on. Turn on. Please, please, Please!* When the vibration stopped, her shoulders sagged, and tears filled her eyes. Somehow, she managed to hold them back, determined not to present a tear-streaked face to her captors. It was a good thing she did.

Amber had no idea how much time had elapsed, but she guessed ten or fifteen minutes when the door once again opened. This time, however, it wasn't the woman. There were two men, and they were carrying someone. Obviously, this wasn't the time to ask for help. This must be the guys who had kidnapped her. She closed her mouth, slumped down, and dropped her head to one side, watching in silence through slitted eyes. Between the two of them was the limp body of an unconscious girl. *That's probably how I was when they brought me here,* Amber thought. *What* is *this place?* Once more, she fought back the tears so she could better focus on the men and the girl.

Without a word, they moved past Amber and then behind her. She could hear them tear duct tape and assumed they were immobilizing the girl, taping her hands and feet just like they had done to her. There was scraping on the floor as they moved the chair with the unconscious girl up directly behind her. Keeping still, head down, Amber felt them stop and stare at her. She held her breath.

"Brought a roommate for you, Princess," one of them sneered.

"She's still out," the other suggested. "Maybe we gave her too much."

"Nah, she'll come out of it. Every one of them reacts differently to the drug. So what if this one takes a little longer. Less hassle for us. Sleep tight, girlies!" He called out laughing as they clumped up the wooden steps.

She waited until she heard the door shut and counted to thirty before daring to open her eyes. They were gone, and the room was totally dark once more, but now she wasn't alone. Someone else was in the room, an unconscious girl, drugged, no doubt, in the same manner as she had been.

Amber started rocking the beach chair, trying to shuffle it around on the concrete floor. The chair moved to the right a fraction of an inch. Shifting the weight in her legs, she actually felt it start to turn. Okay, she could do this. She was about to continue when she heard a noise. She stopped and laid back. The overhead light came on. It was the woman.

Amber sat up and tried to smile but couldn't. She studied the woman as she moved across the room, carrying a tray.

She was less than five feet tall. She had dark hair, cut short with streaks of grey, and walked slightly off-kilter. She didn't limp exactly, but there was something strange about her gait. As she moved closer, Amber studied her face: large brown eyes, a heart-shaped face lined with years of being in the sun. She was Latino, or a mix of that and something else. Amber thought she might have been attractive when she was younger but most likely unable to take advantage of her looks because of her small stature. It was hard to determine her age, perhaps 40, maybe even 50.

"Please tell me who you are and why I'm here. I don't understand any of this."

"Espanol, por favor. No Ingles."

"Oh. I...I don't speak Spanish. Do you speak a little English?"

"No. Espanol, solo."

The woman set the tray down on the floor and, without changing her expression, held up a mug. "Zupa." She held the cup to Amber's mouth. It smelled wonderful, tomato soup with some vegetables. She drank it awkwardly as the woman held it to her lips. She didn't seem hurried or impatient, and periodically, she stopped to give her a sip of another soda and a bite of buttered bread. Amazingly, it was homemade. Surely this meant that she was in the basement of a home. Didn't it?

Who is this woman? Perhaps I can create an ally." She smiled and tried the only Spanish word she knew, "Gracias." Then she continued, "Amber. Am-ber. Me, Amber."

The woman smiled back. "Am-ber," she repeated.

"Yes. Si." She pointed to the woman. "You…your name?"

"Anita." She smiled, and then turned quickly to look back at the door, and then back at Amber with a sad smile. "Mi nombre es Anita."

"Ah, Anita, pretty. Okay, so you don't speak English, but you understand a little."

Suddenly Anita stood up and gathered the things on the tray.

"Please don't leave, Anita. Stay." She motioned with her chin to her taped hands. "Why?"

Anita picked up the tray and then stepped behind Amber to check on the new girl. "Bonito," she murmured and then walked toward the door. She turned. "Adios, Amber."

"Goodbye, Anita."

She now knew exactly where the new girl was behind her. Amber started rocking and shuffling the chair to get close to her. Perhaps together, they could figure out how to escape.

"Hey, hey, hellooo. Can you hear me?" The girl was moving and groaning slightly, but not talking. Amber's right hand now was alongside the girl's hand, side-by-side. Turning her head to look at her, she extended a couple fingers to touch her. If only she would wake up.

"Can you hear me? Can you speak?"

There was a pause and then a grunt.

Amber realized she must have a gag over her mouth. "If you can hear me, I'm a friend. I'm here being held prisoner like you. You probably have a gag in your mouth. If you do, grunt once."

There was a small, frightened grunt.

"Okay. Don't panic. I know this is all scary, but at least there are two of us. You're not alone. It's really dark. We're in a basement somewhere. Do you understand?"

The girl grunted back.

"Alright, I'm going to ask you some questions to see if we can figure this out. Grunt once for yes, twice for no. Ready? My name is Amber. I don't know why I'm here. Do you know why you're here?"

There was a long pause, and Amber wondered if she had slipped into unconsciousness again. Then there was one small grunt.

"You do know? You know why you're here?"

Another grunt.

"Do you know who did this to you?"

The girl grunted again.

"Oh, my goodness. So, you understand all this and…and what's going to happen to us?"

A single sad grunt.

"Are we in danger?"

There was no response because the girl started to sob. And every hope Amber had melted into the darkness. As she listened to the poor girl's wracking sobs, Amber started shaking. The phone began vibrating in her pocket once again. It meant nothing. She would not be found. She would not be rescued. She would not be able to escape the terrible fate that lay in store for her. Amber began to cry.

Chapter Nineteen

Temperature Rising

"This is highly unusual," the middle-aged muscular mall guard said.

"I know," Jon told him. "I know, but listen, my daughter is here somewhere. Her best friend told me so, and she's mad at me. So mad that she is probably hiding so that I can't find her. Please, can we go through that door and check out the employee area just in case?"

The guard glanced at the store clerk.

"I'm telling ya, man. She ain't down there," the young man insisted.

Seeing that the guard was still indecisive, Jon had one last card up his sleeve to play. He had noticed the wedding ring on the man's hand, and he hoped that meant he also had children. "You have any children…" He looked at the name tag on the man's shirt. "…Brian? Any daughters?"

"Three daughters, actually," he replied with a grin. "That's why I'm working this as a second job. I'm a beat cop during the day."

His words brought hope to Jon's heart. "Then, you understand where I am coming from. What if it were one of your daughters? Wouldn't you want to check out every possible situation to find her, especially if you knew she could be in grave danger?"

The look on Brian's face gave Jon his answer. "What's this about being in danger? I don't recall you mentioning that before."

"She has been talking to someone on her computer late at night in secret. I caught her tonight for the second time. I believe this man is not who he claims to be, but a predator looking to kidnap young, innocent girls."

"Why do you think that?" The guard asked.

"Suspicions and bits and pieces of conversation I overheard as well as things her girlfriend said. Amber did not tell her best friend about this guy. Not a peep. Don't you find that the least bit odd?"

"I do," the guard said with a nod. "My girls tell their best friends everything. You said you caught her talking to him again tonight. What happened?"

"She argued with her mother, and I freaked out. The usual teenage stuff, you know what I mean?"

"Indeed, I do," Brian agreed. "My oldest is fourteen and thinks she's all grown up now. She says we spy on her, won't let her do anything, etc. etc." He looked at the sales clerk. "We're checking out the back unless there's some reason you don't want us back there." His words were threatening.

Jon had taken off the glasses, but he put them back on to find a demon whispering furiously into the young man's ear. By the demon's expression and the urgency of its words, it was obvious that it did not want anyone going back there.

As a result, the clerk's reply sounded almost frantic. "No, man, It's just that I could get into a lot of trouble if I leave the store empty. It's more than just the employee area. We keep inventory and stuff back there. When I hired in, the boss said that in no way was I to allow anyone back there."

The clerk's response seemed reasonable, but the nervousness in his voice raised the guard's suspicions. His police training kicked in, and he was confident that the young man was hiding something. "You can stay out here and watch the store. As an off-duty

131

police officer and mall guard, I'm sure your employer will understand why we have to go back there."

Out of excuses and knowing that the guard was becoming suspicious, the clerk returned to stand behind the cash register. The demon disappeared. Brian opened the door and led Jon, who had taken off the glasses, inside to a stock room filled with merchandise. Three entries were visible. One led to a tiny kitchenette with a microwave, a small refrigerator, and a round table with two chairs. The second belonged to a small two-piece bathroom, and the third to a dark staircase that led down to the lower level. A quick check showed the upper-level rooms to be empty.

Brian opened the basement door and turned on the light switch. "Would your daughter go into a dark, unfamiliar basement?"

Jon shook his head no. "She hates basements, especially dark ones. There is no way she would willingly go down there, especially alone."

"Then we'd better check it out."

The two men descended the stairs carefully as the light from the overhead bulb was of low wattage and did not illuminate much of the area around the steps.

"Why would the owner use such a dim bulb here?" Jon asked. "You would think he'd want it brightly lit to prevent anyone from tripping and falling."

"I agree. Let's check it out."

As the guard finished speaking, they heard movement, followed by the sound of something being knocked over. The guard reached for his long-handled flashlight and switched it on.

"Whoever is down here, come out into the light," Brian ordered.

His answer was another scuffling sound, and his hand automatically went to his weapon, his instincts causing him to draw it and point into the darkness toward the sound.

"I am the mall police and an off-duty cop. I have drawn my weapon, so come out now with your hands up, or I'm calling for backup."

****

The door slammed open, but no overhead light was turned on this time. Instead, the beam of a large flashlight lit up the two girls, positioned side-by-side facing each other. For the first time, the two girls could see each other's faces, although the second girl was backlit. They both strained to see each other.

Small and younger than Amber, the girl had blonde hair that hung past her shoulders and chocolate brown eyes that radiated with fear. She had a bruise on one cheek. Her T-shirt, with a Curious George graphic, was ripped at the shoulder. One side of her mouth was bloodied where the gag had cut into her lip. She looked terrified.

"Son of a motherless goat." A tall, bald man crossed the basement floor in seconds to survey the girls. Then he laughed and leaned close to them. "Are you girls having a little pajama party here?"

Amber studied him carefully. What she saw wasn't good. For one thing, he stank of beer mixed with something else disgusting, probably sweat. He had a lascivious smirk on his face and breath that could kill an elephant. She decided to play it tough. Being nice hadn't worked with Anita. So maybe she could bluff her way out of this for both their sakes.

"My dad is on his way here right now with the cops. So, you better let us go. Both of us."

"Really? Your dad, the 'Christian psychiatrist? Oh, he doesn't have a clue where you are. He thinks you ran off with Devon, the skateboard dude. But for Devon and me, we had a deal, and you're it. The deal? Devon will tell him he hasn't seen you in a couple of days and was getting worried himself - maybe send him off on a wild goose chase."

"That's a lie!" Amber yelled.

"I'm afraid not, Princess. And you…" He turned to the other girl, her face smeared with dirty tear streaks. "One of our customers really likes young girls. What are you, Brittany, thirteen, fourteen? And a beauty. He was not disappointed when he met you. Had to delay the delivery, though. You'll go with a bunch of other girls to join your prince."

"You're just full of lies, made up lies," Amber yelled.

Before she could say another thing, the man whipped around and slapped her across the face. "Shut up, you little tart."

Amber's eyes filled with tears of pain and rage. The feeling of helplessness made her want to scream and rip her arms free of their constraints, but she knew that was impossible.

"So, here's the plan, my little cupcakes. You'll get something to eat, and you can visit awhile, but then we'll have to split you up. Tsk, tsk, we'll be sending you two off on different adventures."

The girls' eyes widened in fear when he whipped out a large knife. Then laughing, he cut the tape on each girl's right hand. "So, you can enjoy your last American meal." Then he untied Brittany's gag and threw it on the floor. "I'll see you both later."

He switched on the overhead light as he left, grinning at them while he went through the door. Amber waited a few seconds before speaking.

"Brittany! Let's try to figure something out. Tell me what you know."

"Uh...I was just playing this game online. It's like a fantasy romance site where you pick your character, and you get to play as that character in the game."

"Okay, sounds fun, but why are we here?"

"Shhhh. Listen to me. I'm trying to tell you. In the game, you also have to pick your fantasy partner, like the boy you want to marry. I picked a Saudi-Arabian prince. You know, like in the movie, the girl falls in love with a prince. In fact, I chose the name Jasmine in the game. And it matched me up with another player who chose to be a Saudi-Arabian prince. We got to pretend we were in love, and we went on romantic dates."

"For real?"

"No." Brittany shook her head in frustration. "Online, silly. He kept telling me how beautiful I was, and then after a few weeks, he told me that he really *was* a prince going to a private school here, and he wanted to meet me. I'm only fourteen. I'm not allowed to date yet, but I told him I'd meet him after my ballet class. I told my parents I had a ride home with another girl. He came to pick me up three blocks away from the dance studio."

The girl stopped and again fought back the tears. "He came in a limo with a chauffeur and everything. I couldn't believe it. Then he got out of the backseat and opened the door for me. He said we'd just take a little ride so we could talk, so I got in. It was his voice, and he was so handsome, just like his picture online. I thought I had died and gone to heaven."

"Then what happened?"

"When I got in, he closed the door like he was going to go around to the other side, only he didn't. Heaven became hell. There was another man in the limo, an older man, like my grandpa. And he was wearing a robe. I think he really is a prince or something. He smiled and said, 'You're perfect,' and he nodded. The next thing I knew, I felt a needle in my arm, and then I woke up here."

"Oh, Brittany, I'm so sorry. That's awful."

Amber stopped to take it all in. "Let me think a minute." She sat quietly, and in her mind, she went through everything that had happened to them both. She realized they had been tricked and kidnapped. From her experience with the surfer boy, and with Brittany being lured through a fantasy romance site, she guessed that they were going to be sold through the human trafficking system. Brittany obviously to the Saudi Arabian, and herself? She didn't know. A deep chill sliced through her, making her shiver.

"We have to escape, Brit, before they take us away from here."

"I'm all for that. How?"

The door opened, and Anita entered. "Amber," she called out with a small smile.

"Anita," Amber responded in a friendly tone. Maybe she could convince the woman to help them. "You brought us food, gracias." Anita set down a large tray with two hamburgers, French fries, and two large milkshakes from Mickey D's.

"Por favor, comer"

"She said, please eat."

"You know Spanish?"

"My mom is from Cuba."

"Really? But you're blonde."

"My dad's Norwegian, a mighty Viking." Her eyes filled with tears. "My parents are awesome. I can't believe I did this,"

"Shhh, shhh. We're gonna get out of here." *We have to,* she thought.

"Amber, eat." Anita pointed to the food and then smiled and pointed to Brittany.

"Brit-an-ee," Amber said to the woman.

"Brit-an-ee," she replied.

"Let's eat so Anita can leave."

The girls dug into the food, each using their freed right hand. The cheap hamburger tasted wonderful. No ketchup for the fries, but that didn't matter. As they ate, Anita pulled up a box and sat on it to watch them.

"Brittany, ask Anita why we were brought here. I think we know, but the more information we can get, the better."

"Okay. ¿Senora, Sabes por qué estamos aquí?"

"Bad."

"Bad? What kind of bad? Senora, Somos sólo chicas jóvenes, ¿qué nos pasará?"

"Eat. Terminar"

"¿Tiene hijos?"

Anita did not respond. She just pointed to the food.

"Tenemos madres. Están preocupados. Por favor ayudenos."

"No puedo."

"¿Por qué? Piensa en tus hijas."

Anita stood up. and put the box back. "No mas preguntas. Sólo termine su comida."

Brittany pushed the food away. "No puedo comer, Anita. Estoy muy asustado."

Anita turned away from the girls so that they couldn't see her face.

"What did you say?" Amber asked

"I asked for help and told her to remember her own children, her own daughters. She wouldn't answer, just kept telling me to finish. But I'm not hungry anymore."

Amber, too, had lost her appetite. She sat back in the beach chair. Within moments, the small Latino woman came and picked up their food. Without looking at them, she said softly, "Anita, sorry. Dios sea contigo."

The door closed quietly, and the girls were left alone, again in darkness.

Chapter Twenty

Pray

"Brittany, would you mind if I prayed? I don't know what else to do."

"Please. I believe in God and will pray with you," she said softly.

"I hope he hears us."

"He will. Matthew 18:20 says, 'For where two or three have gathered together in My name, I am there in their midst.'" Brittany assured her.

"Dear Jesus, I'm sorry for not spending much time talking to you. I hope you'll forgive me. It's kind of not fair to ask you to save us, to help us now, but I think...I believe you can if you want to. Please get us out of here. Please send someone to help us. Please. In Jesus' name, Amen."

Amber could hear Brittany crying. Then her phone began vibrating. *Please help my dad find us.* As she said those words in her head, she flashed back to what had started this nightmare and everything her father had said about demonic influence. He had tried to warn her. He had told her mother that they were under attack and when he put those glasses on, he swore he saw a demon on her screen. He saw and heard them plotting not only her own downfall, but the pastor's and the church's as well.

Maybe this whole kidnapping thing is because of demonic influence. How else could anyone be so evil as to want to sell Brittany and me to other evil men as sex slaves? Tears ran down her cheeks. *I thought I was so grown up. I thought my parents were just mean. I'm sorry, daddy. I should have listened to you. Dear Jesus, I promise. If you get us out of this mess, I will never do anything this stupid again.*

****

In the living room upstairs, the men sat around drinking and talking about what they would do with the girls.

"I think we should sample the goods before we sell them," Stinky Francis said, grinning evilly.

"Now that is the stupidest thing you have ever said," the other kidnapper, a white, low life drug dealer named Alan, said. The two men had met in jail several years ago and formed a friendship. "That Saudi guy wants this little girl to be pure and untouched."

Francis emptied his beer bottle and slammed it down on the table next to him. "Anita! Tráeme otra cerveza."

"You need to lay off the beer until we finish this job," Alan warned. "You screw it up now, and we'll lose out on a ton of money."

Anita came into the room, carrying another beer for her husband. Before handing it over, however, she began to argue with him about the girls. Alan knew some Spanish because of his association with the couple, but their words were coming too fast for him to make out all of what was being said. He did recognize enough words, though, to realize that she wanted to let the girls go.

Alan's face became a mask of fury. If Jon had been there with his glasses, he would have seen that both men had demons attached to them. Although what they encouraged their humans to do was in direct conflict, they did it on purpose to create animosity between the men.

After yelling a few words in Spanish to shut them up, he switched to English. "You'd better get that notion out of her head right now. Those girls are worth a fortune, and I plan on getting every penny of it. I got plans for my share."

"Cállate, mujer y saca esa loca idea de tu cabeza," Francis told Anita.

"You'd better tell her more than just to shut up and forget her crazy ideas," Alan warned. His demon whispered in his ear, prompting his next words. "If she helps those girls escape, I'll kill her."

At the other demon's urging, Francis jumped to his feet and lunged at him. "You leave my wife alone. You so much as touch her, and I'll make you wish you had never been born."

The men began throwing punches, slamming into furniture, and knocking over smaller items like the coffee table and a lamp. Fearing for her own safety, Anita threw up her hands and ran from the room, taking the undelivered bottle of beer with her. She had not understood Alan's words, but she knew it was a threat against her by her husband's reaction. Words of fear and prayer escaped her lips as she had so many times in the past, she rued the day her husband had teamed up with Alan. She ended her prayer, begging God to send someone to save the girls being held prisoner in her basement. She was too terrified to help them herself. While her husband might not kill her for helping them, he would beat her senseless, and that wasn't something she wanted to go through again.

****

The mall guard handed his long-handled flashlight to Jon. "Take this and see if you can spot anyone. I'm going to call for backup."

Jon accepted the flashlight and slowly searched the area in front of them. He also put the glasses back on, wondering if the demon from upstairs had come down here when it disappeared. He was so focused on finding something that the guard's voice startled him.

"This is Earl. Come in base."

Static filled the air until another voice replaced it.

"This is base. What's up, Ron?"

"I've got a suspicious situation here in the basement of the Skate Shop, involving a missing girl. Don't know whether she is a runaway hiding so her father won't find her, or if foul play is involved. The father suspects the girl may have been kidnapped."

"Roger that. I'm sending two men your way now."

"Make it three and have one of them secure the male clerk inside the store. He's acting suspicious and may be involved."

"Three it is. Be careful."

"I will." He glanced at Jon. "Anything?"

"Not yet." He continued scanning the area until he spotted a spilled box of inline skates. "Wait, look there."

Earl stepped quietly forward, motioning for Jon to stay behind him. The area around the spilled box was clear, but a scuffle upstairs startled both men. A moment later, two more guards descended the steps.

"Clerk put up a fight?" Earl asked them.

"Tried to make a run for it," one guard replied. "With three to one odds, he didn't stand a chance. What's going on down here?"

"Came down here to investigate. The clerk was acting suspiciously, and we thought we should check down here for the girl. This is her father, by the way." He indicated Jon.

"Dr. Jon Rickner, thank you for your help." He told them about Amber's suspicious online boyfriend. The reason he included his title was so that the mall police would know he wasn't just some crackpot or overzealous father.

"Why don't you wait over by the staircase, Dr. Rickner, while we look around," Earl suggested.

The newly arrived guards pulled out their flashlights and their guns, and the three of them spread out to scour the basement. As they looked around, one man came upon a big rat.

"I think I found your culprit," he told Earl as it scampered into a dark corner.

"It may have knocked over the box, but look what else is down here," Earl said. He had found a small room with a dirty cot and a heavy-duty padlock.

"By the scuff marks in the dirt," one officer said as he pointed to the floor near the cot, "it looks like there was some type of activity here recently.

"We need to clear out, so we don't disturb any evidence," Earl told them. "It's time to call in the local cops."

One man remained outside the room to guard the area, while Earl called the police. The second guard walked over to Jon.

"What did you find? What's in there?" Jon asked frantically.

"Calm down, Dr. Rickner. I'm sorry. I know this is distressing. It looks like something went on here, but we don't know what, and more importantly, we don't know who was involved. It might be nothing, or it might have involved your daughter, but there is no evidence yet to that effect. Why don't we head upstairs and wait for the police to arrive?"

Numb, Jon, preceded the man up the steps. Earl joined them shortly after. They found the other mall guard and the clerk in the small kitchenette. As soon as he saw him, Jon rushed him, grabbing him by the shoulders and shaking him.

"What did you do to my little girl? Where's Amber?"

"I didn't do nothing, man. I swear!"

"That's a lie! If you hurt her...."

As Jon spoke, two police officers walked in. Seeing Earl, whom they both knew, they nodded and walked over to Jon and the clerk. They broke the two men apart and cuffed the clerk after listening to what Earl had to tell them.

As one officer cuffed him, the clerk began to babble.

"I'm tellin' you. I didn't do anything to that girl."

"Ah, so you admit there was a girl," Earl said.

"No...yes."

"Who was she?"

"I don't know," the clerk wailed.

"Yes, he does," Jon said. He pulled out his phone and showed him Amber's picture again. "Was it this girl? Was it my Amber?"

The clerk refused to look, but Earl got tough.

"Look at the picture. Was it that girl?"

Reluctantly, the clerk looked at the picture. It was a stalling tactic. He knew that it was the same girl that it was Amber.

"Yes," he finally admitted. "That's her."

"What did you do to her?" Earl asked.

"I'm tellin' ya. I didn't do nothing."

Looking at him through the glasses, Jon saw that the demon had once more returned. It whispered into the young man's ear. *Don't tell them anything. If you do, you're sunk. You'll go to jail for kidnapping. You'll be blamed for everything that happens to her, and believe me, those will be serious charges. You'll spend the rest of your life in prison.*

The demon's words, however, scared him so much that he wasn't about to shut up. He wasn't going to be blamed for something he didn't do.

"I swear. I didn't do anything. Some guy that hangs around here a lot paid me $500 to leave him and the girl alone in the store for twenty minutes. So, I left and went to the food court for some fries. When I came back, they were gone. I didn't see or hear anything. I'm innocent of any wrongdoing!"

"Some guy?" Earl asked. "Who? If he hangs here all the time, you know his name."

"Devon. Okay? His name is Devon, but I swear I don't know his last name."

"Has Devon ever asked you for this kind of favor before?" one of the other police officers asked.

"No. Never! And...and I told him. I'd do it just this once. Okay."

"You were whining before that you couldn't leave the store unattended, and that was why you didn't want us going downstairs," Earl said. "But your real reason was that you knew about that room downstairs."

"Room? What room?"

His expression of surprise and tone of voice told Earl he was probably telling the truth. Still, he had to press. "You know what room I'm talking about – the room with the dirty cot and the heavy padlock."

"Hey, I knew there was some kind of room down there, but it's always been locked. I swear. I've never seen the inside of it, and I certainly didn't know there was any furniture in it."

"Then why were you so determined not to let us go down there?" Jon asked.

"Man, I'd already left the store unattended once today. I didn't want to take another chance of the owner finding out."

"So why did you do it the first time?" Earl asked.

"Hey, they said it was just for a laugh that nothing would happen to the girl. It was to teach her father a lesson. Besides, I needed the money. There's an awesome new game system out that I want. It's expensive, and there are a couple cool games I want to play on it. $500 would cover it."

Jon looked sick. "So, you traded my daughter's life for some stupid games?"

The demon grinned wickedly at him. His job was done, and he disappeared.

A moment later, as the employee was taken away, the owner of the store walked in. Seeing Earl, he headed straight for him. "What's going on here? I received an emergency phone call from my employee about being arrested because of some kind of prank."

"It would appear that your employee got himself involved with the wrong sort of people."

Suspecting who the man was, Jon approached him. "Are you the owner of this store?"

"I am. What's it to you?"

"I'll tell you what it is to me. You're obviously running some kind of kidnapping ring out of your basement."

The owner flared up with indignation. "Are you crazy? Who is this," he asked the mall guard.

Jon got right into the man's face. "I'll tell you who I am. My daughter, Amber, was drugged and held prisoner in that room of yours downstairs until they took her unconscious body elsewhere."

"Now, there's no proof she was drugged," one of the remaining policemen said.

"Room? What room?"

"Don't act so innocent to me, you child predator. The dark, windowless room with a cot and a lock on the door!"

"Now, hold on just a minute, Dr. Rickner. Give the man a chance to tell his side of the story," Earl said.

"I know of no such room," the owner declared vehemently.

"Oh, come on," Jon snarled. "You own the place. Do you actually expect me to believe that you don't know about that room downstairs?"

The owner opened his mouth to deny it, but then a thought came to him. "There is a small windowless room downstairs with a door and a lock on it. I keep some of the more valuable merchandise in it, but there's no cot in it. Why would there be?"

"Hah, good one, but not good enough. There is no merchandise in there whatsoever. Just a cot to keep drugged kidnapped girls in," Jon countered.

The owner looked at Earl. "Drugged girls? What is he talking about?"

"I'm afraid something went on down there, Mr. Somers. Your employee said it was just a prank, but until we investigate further, we don't know for certain."

Clearly, the only thing that interested the owner was a possible loss of valuable merchandise. "If that room is empty, what happened to the merchandise I kept in there?" He turned to head for the basement door, but Jon reached out and grabbed him roughly.

"I'm not falling for that line of malarkey. What's a matter? Not earning enough in the store that you started kidnapping girls and selling them as sex slaves?"

"You're crazy. Take your hands off me."

"Not until you tell me what you did with my little girl!"

The two men struggled until Jon hauled off and decked the owner in the nose, breaking it.

Earl and one of the other policemen stepped in and separated the two.

"There, now, that's enough of that," Earl said.

Pulling out a handkerchief to stem the flow of blood, the owner turned to the on-duty policeman. "I want that man arrested for assault. Once I close the store for the night, I'll come down to file charges."

Earl tried to defuse the situation. "Hold on, Mr. Somers. It is possible that Dr. Rickner's daughter was taken and held prisoner in that room. Surely you understand why he is so upset."

"He may be upset, but that doesn't give him a reason to attack me. I want him arrested," Somers insisted.

"I'm sorry, Dr. Rickner, but I have to place you under arrest," the policeman said as he cuffed him.

"No, I don't have time for this. I have to find my daughter," Jon said, struggling.

"Now, just take it easy," Earl said.

Jon wouldn't listen. He continued to struggle, forcing the two officers to pin him to the ground and cuff him. Once they brought him back to his feet, the fight had gone out of him, but the arresting officer wasn't finished yet.

"Should the man's suspicions prove correct, you will need to come down and answer some questions as well, Mr. Somers. That room is suspicious, and if what he says happened, there actually did, you are going to have a lot of explaining to do."

Aside from the clerk's confession, however, there was no definite proof that anything devious had happened. The girl and possibly her boyfriend just might have been playing a prank on her father. Until they learned the truth, nothing was certain.

Chapter Twenty-One

Amber and Brittany

Amber must have drifted off to sleep because she jerked upright when the shouting and fighting erupted upstairs. Once more, she wondered if the men weren't under the influence of demons. Knowing it had something to do with them, she decided to use their distraction to their advantage.

"Brittany. Are you awake?"

"Uh-huh."

"They forgot to tape our right hands up again. Let's try to at least get our left hands and feet free. Maybe we can tear the tape off." Both girls started working on their left hands, looking for the end of the tape, or a weak spot.

"I found the end!" Brittany whispered loudly. Even though their chances of being overhead were low, due to all the noise upstairs, she thought it better not to risk it. "I can pull it back. It's coming."

Amber was having more difficulty. *The end may be tucked under another piece of tape,* she thought. Then she found it. Within a few minutes, they each had unraveled the tape. With both hands free, they bent over and worked on their ankles.

Amber was free first and crouched next to Brittany to help free her other leg. When that was done, they stood on shaky legs and hugged each other.

"We need to reshape the duct tape so we can lay it over our wrists and ankles to make it look like we're still attached in case someone comes in," Amber said.

The girls worked on it in the dark, shaping the tape around one hand and both ankles, until they were satisfied it would pass if someone came in to check on them.

Although they didn't know it, two hours had passed. They were due for another inspection.

"What now, Amber?"

"I did some looking around when the light was on, and Anita was here. I saw some high windows over on that wall. They're painted over, so maybe we can scratch a message through the paint and someone outside will see it. Let's try that."

The girls blindly felt their way across the basement, feeling up the walls until Brittany called out, "Here's one!" It was too high for them to reach, so Amber pulled a small box over. Deftly she hoisted herself on top of it.

"I can reach it," she said triumphantly, "but I need something sharp. My fingernails won't scratch through the paint."

Brittany began to search the dark basement, hands outstretched, hoping to come upon something with an edge until she realized that something had changed. "It's awfully quiet upstairs."

"You're right. We better hurry."

A new sound sent both girls scrambling toward their chairs. Brittany reached hers first and placed the tape over her ankles and one over her left hand. Amber barely made it when the door opened. The flashlight came on, and the stinky bald man entered. He threw the beam of light across the girls when he reached the end of the staircase. They blinked.

"Ha! So, you rearranged the furniture in your suite, eh? Why's that?" He stepped closer, pointing the flashlight first at their left hands, and then down toward their feet.

"We wanted to be next to each other," Amber offered meekly. The last thing she wanted to do was to get the man angry.

151

"Really?" The big man started moving toward them.

"Francis!" A voice called from the top of the staircase.

Francis?

The girls looked at each other. It was funny, but they didn't dare laugh.

"Francis, you better get up here. We got trouble."

The man stopped halfway across the room. "You girls behave yourselves. Keep the party noise down to a minimum." He laughed, made one more pass around the room with the flashlight, and turned toward the door.

"Francis!" Alan appeared in the doorway.

"What is so freakin' important?"

"Cops!"

Hope surged in the girls' minds. *Cops!*

Stinky Francis bounded up the stairs two at a time and angrily slammed the door so hard it bounced against the frame but remained open. Neither man noticed as they hurried to deal with their trouble.

The girls waited for several minutes.

"Brittany, go over to the door and listen. See if you hear them talking. I'm going to try for the window again. Maybe a cop will see our message or hear me tapping on the window. As Amber moved toward the window, she ran her hand along the boxes and shelves in the room. There was more light now, and she spotted a screwdriver. Perfect. Quickly she picked it up and climbed on top of the box to the window.

She listened for noise outside, nothing. She pushed hard with the screwdriver and wrote HELP. KIDNAP.

"Amber," Brittany whispered from the doorway. "The cops are asking questions. But I can't understand the words."

"Keep listening." Amber continued with the screwdriver, one more word. BASEMENT. Amber tried to lift the window. It was too small to climb out, but she could yell for help. It didn't budge. But now she heard voices from the house.

"They're arguing. I think the cops left. But I can hear them yelling."

"I heard a car start up," Amber responded, from her position near the window. Moments later, she heard another car start. "What do you hear now, Brit?"

"It got real quiet. I don't hear anything."

Amber climbed down from the box and made her way toward Brittany and the open door. Surveying the basement once again in the extra light.

"I think they left. Maybe the cops scared them off?" The girls looked at each other. Could they escape? This would be the time.

"Don't stand up. Crawl." They inched their way across the basement door threshold and into the other room. It was a laundry room. When they got to the closed door, Amber stood and turned the doorknob ever so slowly, then cracked the door. Brittany held her breath. Amber peeked through the crack. Empty kitchen. She returned to the floor.

"Come on." The girls opened the door enough to crawl through and closed it behind them, then moved across the kitchen floor. There was an outside door to the left. Their hearts beat so loudly, they were sure they could be heard. They crawled toward the door.

Amber retook the lead, and slowly raised her head to look out of the kitchen door window. They were in the country, a big field spread before them, a cornfield. She moved her eyes left to right. No one.

"Let's go." Amber pushed the door open and crawled out, Brittany right behind her. Slowly they stood, then made a mad dash for the cornfield. Neither looked back, but ran like Olympic track stars, eyes on the goal - corn! Brittany actually passed Amber and reached the field first. But Amber was right on her heels. About twenty feet into the corn, they both slowed down to a reasonable trot, pushing corn stalks out of their way.

Halfway across, Amber stopped. "Let's rest, Brit. We may have to run when we get to the other side, and we want to save our strength."

"I can't stop. I can slow down, but don't make me stop," Brittany replied.

"Alright, let's go."

"What's on the other side?"

"I don't know. I hope a road."

Within ten minutes, they reached the end of the field, and a narrow strip of asphalt lay before them.

Brittany turned to Amber, "Which way should we go?"

"I don't have any idea where we are, except in the country. We should just start walking, I guess. Maybe we'll see a sign."

"What time do you think it is?"

"I'm guessing four or five o'clock, judging by the sun. I hope we can find help before dark. We'd better start walking."

They started out, walking on the road, but close to the field.

"Did you hear that?"

"No. What?"

"Someone in the cornfield behind us."

"Run, Amber whispered, on the road."

Without hesitation, the girls began to run. The corn behind them rustled, someone was running in the cornfield.

"A car!" Brittany yelled, "behind us."

"Flag it down. . . jump in the road."

The girls ran to the center of the road and waved their arms frantically. When the headlights hit them, the car came to a screeching stop just feet away. They ran to the car, as the driver's door opened, and straight into the arms of stinky Francis.

Both girls screamed and turned to run. But he grabbed Brittany by the hair, then around the waist, and threw her in the back seat of the car, where tiny little Anita sat, with a gun.

Amber stopped, and then realized she couldn't help Brittany, she had to get away and took off.

Francis cursed as he chased after her. He was gaining. She turned back into the cornfield. Maybe she could lose him there. She wove in and out, trying to work her way back to the road, praying for another car, and that Francis wouldn't catch her. She stopped. Where was he? She didn't hear him. Maybe he was far enough behind her that if she went slowly, she could lose him. Besides, she was out of breath. She would trick him. *Just stay still, wait for him to move.* Amber hunkered down to the ground, making herself small and attempted to control her breathing. *Quiet, quiet, quiet,* she thought.

It was getting dark now. She'd been sitting in the same place for almost an hour. It was time to move. She was sure the kidnappers had given up and gone back to the house. Slowly Amber started to crawl along the ground toward the road or where she thought the road was. She wanted to get up and run, but her instincts told her not to; stay low, go slow.

The corn started to thin out, and she could feel the ground start to change. She was close, close to the road. She would stay in the cornfield, but next to the road. She listened. No cars. *Stand up, Amber, get moving. They have Brittany, you have to get help. You can't stay in the cornfield. You have to go for help.* Amber stayed to one side as she walked down the road.

She smelled him just seconds before he grabbed her from behind.

"Did you really think you could get away?" He breathed angrily into her ear. "You'll pay for this. Just wait." With an iron grip on her arm, he walked her across the road to a motorcycle parked a few hundred feet down the road. "Get on, Princess."

"But I've never. . ."

"You'll learn, or you'll fall off. Get on?"

Amber straddled the bike, and the horrible man got on behind her. His filthy body leaned into her, the smell making her gag. His long arms reached around Amber's side and grasped the handlebars.

"You know, Princess, it would be a lot easier to just kill you. But I don't want to be that kind."

Chapter Twenty-Two

A Night in Jail

Inside a small glass interrogation room, Jon sat at a long metal table in a metal chair with black cushions on the seat and back. Across from him were two detectives in dark suits, dress shirts, and ties. The lead detective, Leo Sandburg was a short, stocky no-nonsense type of guy and an extreme skeptic. He had interviewed the worst of the worst, and it was difficult for him to believe anything unless it was what he wanted to hear.

The second detective, Jason Miller, was a practicing Christian. Tall and thin with a pleasant demeanor, he often played good cop compared to his partner's bad cop. Typically, two detectives would not be involved in a simple assault case, which was what had brought Jon into the station in the first place. Once the officers from the scene had explained the extenuating circumstances of the alleged kidnapping of Jon's daughter, however, these two night-shift detectives were called in.

Jon was upset and nervous. This was the last place he wanted to be. "Listen, fellows, can we make this short? I have to get back out there and look for my daughter." He glanced at his watch. "I need to find her before it's too late."

"How old is your daughter?" Detective Miller asked.

"She's fifteen."

The detectives exchanged a look.

"Fifteen, and she's been gone how long?" Detective Miller asked.

Jon looked at his watch. "Six hours."

Detective Sandburg looked disgusted. "Six hours?" He threw his hands up in the air. "And they called us in for this?"

"Wait just a minute, Leo. According to the officers from the scene, there's more to it than just a teenager for missing six hours. It's a suspected abduction."

Sandburg wasn't convinced. "So, what's this about? Did you have a fight with your daughter - a misunderstanding?"

Jon was so tired of going over the story. "Yes, and she ran off to the mall to meet some boy. I haven't been able to reach her by phone or text."

"She's a teenager. Her battery probably ran out," Sandburg said.

"No. She wouldn't do that. She's a responsible girl." Jon was totally frustrated.

No one said anything for a couple minutes.

"What was the argument about?" Miller asked.

"Her secretly communicating with some boy she didn't know over the internet."

"Kids these days," Sandburg said, "that's what they do."

"It wasn't just a boy. It was a…a man pretending to be a boy her age…a predator."

"How do you know that?" Miller inquired.

"I just know," Jon replied.

"So it might be a predator, or it just could be some young guy looking to find a girlfriend," Sandburg complained. "You've got no proof one way or the other."

"Look, you're asking me these questions, wasting time. Just trust me that I know she's in trouble."

"Well, Jon, we'd like to trust you, but you haven't given us anything to trust in. So far, it's all your interpretation. What we do know is that you created a disturbance in the mall. You trespassed on private property. You accosted the owner, and you resisted

158

arrest. That's what we know. If you can tell us more, we would appreciate it," Miller told him.

"Okay. Forget it. I just want to get out of here. I'll try to find Amber myself."

"We just can't let you go, Jon. We're concerned you may hurt someone else," Sandburg said.

"I haven't hurt or threatened anyone," Jon insisted.

"On the contrary, you threatened Mr. Somers and punched him in the face," Sandburg growled. "That's assault. You also resisted arrest. For all I know, as soon as you get out of here, you might go after him again and really hurt him this time."

"I wouldn't do that." Jon's shoulders sagged. He was so tired of trying to convince people of things that no one believed because they couldn't see and hear what he did. Now, however, he felt compelled to tell them about the spiritual element.

"As it was explained to me, we are in a spiritual battle of good against evil, and it's worse than most of us imagine. Whether or not we decide to participate in that battle is a choice each person has to make." He saw the skepticism on Sandburg's face. "Look at it this way. As police officers, I'm sure you have seen some heinous things on the job. Haven't you ever stopped and wondered how a person could do those things to someone else? Haven't you ever felt somewhat overwhelmed by it – the inhumanity of it all?"

Miller leaned forward, intrigued. Those thoughts had plagued him more frequently than he would like. Regardless of their reasons for doing it, he would never understand why people did some of the things they did.

Sandburg wasn't having any of it. "The bad guys do what they do because they are greedy, selfish, and enjoy hurting others." He turned to his partner. "Give him a sobriety test. You take any medication?"

"No," Jon replied. "And I drink very little."

Miller didn't believe for a minute that Jon was drunk. Nevertheless, he said. "Take the sobriety test, just to prove to my partner that you aren't drunk."

"Fine. Let's get it over with."

Miller stepped outside the room, returning a moment later with a uniform officer, who gave Jon the test.

"Negative," the officer said when he finished.

"Not even close?" Sandburg asked in disbelief.

"Nada, zero, zip, zilch."

"Okay, okay, I get it."

"Maybe we should give your wife a call," Miller said.

"No, she is at the hospital with her mother and doesn't know our daughter is missing. I don't want to alarm her."

"But you want us to go looking for your daughter," Miller said.

"Yes."

"Did you and your wife have an argument? Would your daughter be upset because of it?" Sandburg asked.

"No. This has nothing to do with our argument."

"Then, you did have an argument." Sandburg practically jumped on him verbally.

"We argued over our daughter's behavior, but that isn't what caused her to run out."

"Then why are you so sure she disappeared?" Miller asked.

"Someone told me."

"Who?" Sandburg asked.

"It was a voice."

"You hear voices? How often?" Sandburg smiled, thinking that now he was getting somewhere.

"It's not like that. I know where this voice comes from."

"And where does it come from?" Miller asked gently.

"You'll think I'm crazy. I'm not. I'm a well-respected psychiatrist."

"Then tell us whose voice it is," Miller said encouragingly. "Is it God's voice?"

"I wish."

"Okay, Dr. Rickner, then whose voice is it? Is it all in your head?" Sandburg wanted to know.

"No. It's an actual voice. When I put on these glasses," Jon began as he pulled them from his pocket, "I can see creatures and hear their voices. They're evil. Demonic."

The detectives looked at each other. They didn't respond. Sandburg was expressionless, but Miller looked interested.

"Can we see those glasses?" Miller asked.

Jon started to hand them to Miller, but Sandburg grabbed them out of his hand.

"You see and hear demons when you put these on?" He asked, stifling a smirk.

"Yes, but not all the time. They have to be present. None are here right now."

Sandburg put on the glasses and looked around. Nothing. As he removed them, the smirk escaped.

Miller took them from him and inspected them, examining the frames, etc. "And these demons are telling you that your daughter is in trouble?"

"Yes! She's been abducted. She was at the mall, at that Surf and Skateboard Shop. I saw her headband in the backroom. She was there."

"A headband? It could have been anyone's," Miller said, trying to reason with him.

"It was her 'lucky' headband. She was there."

Sandburg took the glasses from his partner and put them in his pocket.

"Can I have my glasses back?" Jon asked, extending his hand.

"If you are seeing demons and hearing voices, maybe you shouldn't have them."

"Give 'em back, Leo. You've got no right to keep them," Miller said, taking them back and handing them to Jon.

"So, what's next?" Jon asked. "Can I go look for my daughter now?"

"We have to check something out first," Miller replied. He wanted to get his partner out of the room to discuss a few things in private. They left Jon alone in the room with only his thoughts.

The detectives did not go far. They stood on the other side of the one-way mirror and watched as they talked. Jon put the glasses on and looked around. Nothing. Then Slipknot walked through the one-way glass, wearing an evil grin.

Knowing that they could be watching him, Jon tried not to react, but he was so startled that he could not hide the horrified expression on his face. Desperation drove him to speak, but he kept it to a whisper.

"What do you want? Where's Amber?"

The two detectives went back and forth about whether or not Jon was crazy until they see him arguing with what appeared to be empty space.

"Lock him up and let the shrinks sort it out in the morning," Sandburg said, disgusted. "I'm going back to work on a real case."

Alone, Miller came back in.

"Look, Officer, I understand you can't start a search until she's missing for 24 hours. If you're a father, you'll understand that I can't wait that long. I believe she's in danger. Just tell me how I can get out so I can try to find my daughter."

"Actually, that's not true, especially in the case of a child. If there is a reason to suspect that a child has been abducted, an AMBER alert can be filed immediately." The detective looked at Jon, studying him. "I have two daughters of my own."

"Then you should understand. What would you do if one of your girls was missing?"

"Whether it's true, or not, that my daughter's in trouble, that doesn't change what I believe. If you were in my place, could you just stand by and do nothing? Or would you go looking for your little girl? I just want to get out of here, so I can find her. Maybe she's okay, and this is just…whatever. Like the other guy said, she's a teenager, but let me out to search for her. If she has been abducted, as I suspect she has…" Jon left the sentence unfinished.

Miller was inclined to believe him, or at least he was willing to try. He knew it was possible. Another officer, sent by Sandburg, came into the interrogation room, took Jon by the arm, and led him through the door.

"Gotta spend a little time with us, buddy."

Miller and Jon talked as they walked down the barren hallway.

"Do me a favor," Jon said. "Interrogate that store clerk they brought in earlier, the one who said that my daughter was just playing a trick on me with some guy to teach me a lesson. I know that isn't true. Amber would never do something like that. The guy admitted he was in on it."

"Alright, I will. If, after interrogating him, I'm convinced that your daughter has been abducted, I'll issue an Amber Alert and start the ball rolling. But until that happens, I'm afraid you are stuck here for the night."

Chapter Twenty-Three

A Long Night

Jon was locked in a cell with three guys with demon tattoos. He wondered if they were in his daughter's abduction until he mentally shook himself. They weren't. They couldn't be. Three were tattooed biker types. One had a giant skull tattooed on his arm. They looked him up and down. Two turned away.

The third guy was talkative, Mr. Personality. "You look like a preacher or a banker. What'd ya do?"

"Do? I'm a psychiatrist."

"No. Why ya in here?"

"Uh, I think I'm charged with assault, and uh maybe destroying property. I'm not sure. Oh, and resisting arrest. I guess that's it. Can you be charged with crazy? Cause I think that might be in there as well."

"Nope. I don't think that's a legal charge. Not sure, though," the guy replied. "You're not drunk or high, so why'd you do all that?"

"My daughter, she's been abducted."

The other two bikers turned around and started listening.

"When?"

"Sometime this evening." Jon banged on the cell bars in frustration. "Cops won't do anything!"

"Yeah, she's a teenager. They probably figure she just ran away," Mr. Personality said.

"Right. Well, while they're trying to figure out if she's been kidnapped or not, Amber is in terrible danger. I have to get out of here and go find her."

"You know who grabbed her?"

"No, but I know where The Skate Shop at the Mall."

The other two bikers look at each other and walked over.

"Paradise Surf & Skate?"

"Yes. You know them?"

One guy turned away, the other answered. "Maybe. How old is she?"

"Just turned sixteen recently."

"Shit."

"What do you mean?"

"You're right, she's in trouble. Those guys that run that shop…not good."

"Tell me," Jon begged.

"Shut up, Wayne."

"Hey, the guy's got a daughter missing. What if someone took Rebel? Huh?

The man was silent. He turned away. The other two watched him. It was apparent he was their leader.

"Listen, what's your name?"

"Jon. Jon Rickner."

"Jon. If she's mixed up with those guys at the shop, ya gotta get out of here."

"Yeah? How? I haven't even had a phone call yet."

The two bikers started yelling and rattling the cell bars.

"Hey! Hey! Got an emergency here! Somebody come help!"

Miller and another cop with keys rushed in. "What's going on? Somebody hurt?"

"We got a situation here."

"What?" The officer on duty asked.

The one in charge stepped forward from the back of the cell. "He said we got a situation here."

The cops looked at the intimidating biker. "What is it?"

"This man, his daughter's been abducted. That ain't good. Since you guys aren't doing anything to save her, you should let him out, so he can find her."

"Why are you?"

"Look, that place she was taken from, lots of girls have disappeared from there. You gonna help this man, or ya gonna live with the knowledge that you could have saved his daughter from a fate worse than death and didn't. Cause I sure as hell will pass it around to my friends and acquaintances. Most of em are daddies, too. Go get your boss. Let this man go."

The jailer turned toward the detective, who saw the desperation in Jon's eyes. Things were beginning to add up.

"No need Eli, I'll take care of it. You know someone who can come down and post bail?"

"Yes, my friend and business partner."

"Come on, Dr. Rickner. Let's call your friend and get him over here."

"Thank you."

The three bikers nodded. One gave him a thumb up, but Eli, the leader, had already turned and walked to the back corner of the cell.

167

The jailer shut and locked the cell door. "Danny, Zooter, Eli, You did the right thing. G'night."

****

Ten detective desks, all side by side, fill a rundown room. Half have detectives sitting at them. Phones and computers were busy with activity.

Detective Miller walked over the Sergeant's desk to convince him that Jon was harmless and should be allowed to leave.

The lead cop opens the file. "No record. The drug test is clean. He's sober. He even belongs to the Police Athletic Booster Club. Alright."

"Course, with these charges, you'll have to post bail, Dr. Rickner."

"My friend, He'll do that for me. Please.

The cop nods his head, "Alright, you can make your call and post bail.

"Thank you, officer." Jon points to the officer's jacket. "Can I please have my glasses back?"

"Oh," He pulls them out of his pocket, holds them up and peers through them again, shakes his head, and hands him glasses."Are you sure?"

"Yes."

"Take him to the other room. He can wait there. Get his personal belongings and give em back. And Dr. Rickner. . ."

"Yes, sir."

"Call us in sixteen hours if you haven't found her."

****

Chapter Twenty-Four

The Countdown

Jon drove home in a state of numbness. He had seen news stories where someone had murdered, beaten, or robbed another person for reasons as illogical and simplistic as this. However, he had never dreamed that something like this would ever happen to his family or anyone he knew for that matter. His last words kept rattling around in his head like a metal ball swirling around a toilet before finally flushing down the drain. *You traded my daughter's life for some stupid games?*

The police had tried to reassure him. They would do everything they could to find Amber and return her safely to her family. In the meantime, he should return home in case there was a ransom call, however unlikely that might seem. Detectives would be in contact with him there.

When he arrived home, he realized that his wife had not yet returned, and it hit him. She had no idea that Amber had been kidnapped. Should he call and tell her? He would have to eventually but not over the phone. Right now, Brooke needed to be with her ailing mother. There was nothing she could do here to help. *She'll probably be angry with me for not telling her sooner.* It was something he would deal with when the time came. For now, he had to concentrate on what to do next.

Jon entered the house and ran up the steps to Amber's room. It was eerily dark except for the feeble light still emanating from his daughter's wrecked computer. He crossed the room to where the broken laptop lay in the corner where he had kicked it earlier. He bent down and picked it up. Then he carried it over to her desk and set it on top.

Although the screen was still in one piece, the glass was fractured in two places with small spider web type circles the size of a silver dollar. Jon put on the glasses and sat in front of the computer. The screen was blank. Access to the site she had been on had been terminated. *Why wouldn't it be?* He thought. They had her, so her access to the site was no longer needed. He stared at the glaring light for several moments, his mind a blank as to what he should do next. Then he had an idea. *I should check her email. That must be how he contacted her.*

Clicking the X to close the page, he reopened the internet to her email page and began going through her mail, reading several that she had written. It was more a feeling that crept upon him. Jon felt the hair on the back of his neck rise, and an icy chill run down his spine. He shivered. It was as though someone had walked on his grave. Then he noticed what appeared to be a shadow reflected in the computer screen. Even though it wasn't clear, he knew what he was seeing.

"I know you're there," Jon said, turning to face the demon.

"Ah, the glasses! Those glasses may reveal us, but they do not reveal our power and authority."

"All power and authority comes from God," Jon said, quoting scripture.

Slipknot's face went blank at first, but then he changed the subject. "We can end all of this."

"This?"

The demon laughed. "Come now, Jon. Your daughter is in trouble – deep serious trouble. You put up a good fight, but you never had a chance."

Jon fought to keep from showing his anguish. This wasn't over yet. Somehow, he had to find a way to defeat the demon and get his daughter back. "So, now what? Are you here to torment me by giving me the sordid details of what will happen to her?"

"While that would give me no end of delight, I'm actually here to offer you a deal. Give up the glasses."

"And if I do?"

"If you do, we will see that she is returned to you unharmed."

A million things ran through Jon's mind. His first encounter with the glasses. His realization that they really worked and weren't just a figment of Carson's imagination. Learning about the war being waged and his acceptance to join the fight. Meeting Paul Haas, the bookstore owner, and the downward spiral that followed. *I didn't want to join this fight,* he thought. *I wanted to pretend it didn't exist, or that I could never play a worthwhile part in it. And now that I know… Can I give it up, even to save my own daughter?*

"Why? Why me? Why Amber? Why, after all these years, did you decide to attack my family? And why the glasses?"

"Because before you didn't matter. At all. You didn't do anything to bother or interfere with our mission. You bought some fire insurance for eternity. Well, that's what you thought anyway. You were 'saved' from…I don't know…Hell? Ha. Ha. Ha. Ha."

Its laugh was like fingernails on a chalkboard to Jon. He winced. "That changed when I discovered the glasses and their power."

"It wasn't finding the glasses that did it. You could have gone through life observing what we were doing, and nothing would ever have happened. It was when you started nosing around, trying to make a difference, trying to change how we do things here that brought you to our attention."

Slipknot moved closer, his demeanor turning darker and more foreboding, threatening. "What you don't understand, Jon is that My Lord rules this world. My Lord makes the decisions. My Lord controls your life. When you interfere with any of his plans, he does not like it. You will suffer the consequences. My Lord decides what happens to you and your family. Everything, Jon. Everything!"

Jon shook his head, rejecting the demon's words. "No, God rules the world. God decides what happens. He determines…"

"What, Jon?" Slipknot roared. "What *exactly* does He do? He gives you free will – free will that He will not intervene with. My Lord has no such restrictions. He has free rein to do as he wishes. By chance, do you know who gave it to him? God!"

Jon was stunned to silence. It was true. Every word and it left him shaken to his very core. At any other time, he might remember that God would intervene and help when called upon. He would send his angels to aid you, but in his current state of mind, Jon forgot all that. He felt beaten, abandoned, helpless.

Seeing how effective his words had been, the demon backed off, his expression changing to appear almost friendly.

With a crooked smile, he said, "fortunately for you, I have the authority to negotiate some terms with you - to strike a bargain. I can either save Amber or destroy her slowly, painfully. The choice will be yours. The glasses? Well, they're just a nuisance for us. Your looking into our world is disturbing. We don't like it. For you, the glasses have brought you nothing but pain. So, here's my offer. Give up, destroy, bury, throw away the glasses where they will never be found, and I will return Amber to you - unharmed. That's it. You want Amber back, we want the glasses destroyed. A simple exchange of favors."

"It seems too simple. In fact, it seems like maybe the glasses are worth more than you're telling me that they affect more of your power than you're willing to admit. I believe they're more than a nuisance." Jon seemed to rally back, but in truth, his words sounded more like those of an automaton.

"Really, Jon? You would trade your daughter's life for a pair of glasses? How do you think Brooke would feel about that? Oh, really, that is rich! I can just hear you explain it to your wife. 'Like my glasses, honey? Yeah, I know Amber suffered a horrible death, but they make me look good.' Ha, ha, ha, ha, ha. I don't think she'll understand your decision."

"So, you're telling me that you will return Amber, unharmed if I get rid of these glasses? That's the exchange?"

"Jon, let's be honest, you haven't always made the right decisions by Amber. This one…you can't blow it."

The computer turned on, and Jon whipped around to view a montage of him making a bad decision with Amber. A slew of bad decisions that reminded him that he was not only an imperfect parent but that at times when he placed his needs above those of his family, he was unjust, even cruel. The video played, and Jon watched it horrified. Slipknot appeared next to the computer.

"Get rid of the glasses, Jon, forever, destroyed, never to be discovered again. Then we'll return Amber, unharmed. Yes, that's my offer. And Jon, I wouldn't wait too long to agree. We have very little patience, you know, and Amber is in a precarious –actually, a life or death situation. You better make your decision soon - and the right one." The demon disappeared.

Jon's eyes were drawn back to the computer that immediately switched scenes. He saw Amber in the basement, tied up. Her phone vibrated and she screamed out, 'Daddy!'

The demon said that, at some point, very soon, I will run out of patience, so you better make your decision soon.

Jon stood up confused.

As soon as you get rid of glasses, we will release your daughter from men who have no idea they are working for us.

****

A knock on the front door snapped him out of his funk. *Oh, God, please let it be Amber.* He ran down the steps to the entrance, hoping beyond hope that somehow his daughter had escaped and found a way to return home. He threw open the door, and hope died as quickly as it had sprung up. Standing there was Detective Fred Behnken, and this is my partner, Detective Angie Morehouse.

"Dr. Rickner," Detective Behnken said. "May we come in?"

Jon closed his eyes briefly, hoping that when he opened them, he would see the one he had so fervently prayed would be there.

She wasn't.

Without saying a word, he stepped back and allowed the two detectives to come inside.

"We had hoped we wouldn't have to make this call, but it seems my partner, Det. Morehouse and I were correct in our assumptions."

Jon's face turned ashen. "Amber! She's not…She's not..." He couldn't bring himself to say the word he dreaded so much.

"Oh, no, Dr. Rickner," Det. Morehouse said. "As far as we know, your daughter is still okay." *Or at least as okay as she can be in this situation.*

Jon's legs trembled, and for a moment, it looked as though he would collapse until Det. Behnken grabbed his arm to steady him.

"I'm sorry, sir," Det. Morehouse said. "We didn't mean to scare you."

"Then what are you doing here?" Jon was bewildered. "You were checking into Carson's suicide."

"Yes, and we were about to close that case when we heard about your daughter's kidnapping," Det. Behnken told him. "Normally, we only do homicide, but there has to be a connection. So, we did a lot of talking to the Lieutenant and were given permission to come on board."

Jon shook his head in frustration. "No, there is no connection. You don't understand. Carson committed suicide. He wasn't murdered." But a little voice inside his head rang out like a death knoll.

Are you sure?

"You've thought of something?" Det. Behnken asked.

"No." He shook his head again. There was indeed a connection, but not one that the police could follow up on. Plus, they would never believe him. "These people who kidnapped Amber, why would they care about killing a man who had no connection with us whatsoever?"

"Until he became your patient," Det. Morehead said. "Is it possible that he told you something they didn't want to be known? Something that got him killed and your daughter kidnapped to keep you quiet?"

Jon wished that he was an accomplished actor because he could not control the look on his face or body language that told the detectives that they were on to something. How could he? These detectives had hit the nail on the head, but what they did not realize was that it wasn't the men involved that made the connection. It was the demons.

"No, I'm convinced that Carson killed himself." He looked at the two detectives and asked, "Have you found any evidence that proves otherwise?"

"No," Det. Morehead admitted. "But that doesn't mean it didn't happen." When she saw that Jon was about to reject the idea again, she quickly continued. "Look, we're on the case, so why not let us do our job? When all is said and done, if we find no connection, then we'll write off Carson's death as a suicide and leave it at that. In the meantime, we need to find whoever has your daughter and rescue her."

"What do you need from me?" Jon asked.

"Everything," Det. Behnken replied. "By the way, where is your wife?"

"She's at the hospital. Her mother collapsed this evening just before Amber ran away. She knows that Amber ran off, but she doesn't know about the kidnapping. I was about to leave for the hospital to tell her when you arrived here."

"Then we'll try to do this as quickly as we can, but we need to tell us what you know."

Jon told them everything, leaving out only the parts the demons played. They went over the painful scene that had sent Amber running from the house, his discussion with her best friend, and what had happened at the mall. He also gave them his daughter's computer. They would put one of their tech people on it to see if they could trace the website as well as the emails she had exchanged with her kidnapper. By the time they finished up, quite a bit of time had passed, and Jon was exhausted. Reliving the experience had been almost as bad as going through it originally.

Det. Morehouse placed a hand on Jon's shoulder. "Don't give up hope. We'll be calling the Feds in on this, and between us, we'll run it through everything we can throw at it. We'll find her, Dr. Rickner."

As soon as they pulled out of the driveway, Jon left for the hospital. It was time to tell Brooke.

Chapter Twenty-Five

Parental Discretion

Jon found Brooke in her mother's room, both asleep; Margaret snored quietly, her monitor creating a quiet, steady beep in the background. Across the room, Brooke lay on a recliner, a thin white blanket tucked around her, one small foot peeking out. He wasn't going to wake her, but she stirred, sensing him in the room, and she looked up.

"Jon?"

"Hi, sweetheart." He smiled as he crossed the room. Brook sat up straighter and scooted her legs to the side, thinking he might sit down. Instead, he gently ran his fingers through her hair. She looked beautiful to him.

"I didn't know you were…"

"Shhh." Jon pulled her up from the edge of the chair and embraced her with a strength that took her breath away. She could feel his love, tender and sure, and she silently allowed herself to be drawn in.

"I love you, Brooke," he whispered, and then he pushed her slightly away to look into her eyes. "I've been unfair to you, keeping you out, when what I wanted desperately was to include you and be open about everything."

"Jon, what is it? What are you talking about?"

"A couple of things, actually. First and most importantly, I need to tell you about Amber."

The tone of his voice alerted her to the fact that all was not well.

"What about Amber? Is she home? Is she still upset? Did the two of you work things out?"

"Brooke, Amber has been kidnapped."

His wife's eyes grew large with anguish. "Kidnapped? But how? Why? We don't have the kind of money kidnappers usually want."

"She went to meet that boy at the mall. He wasn't there, but the sales clerk was in cahoots with some bad people."

Brooke's knees began to buckle, but Jon stepped in and held her securely. "Was it the one on the computer she was talking to?"

"Yes."

"And has there been a ransom demand?"

"Not yet, but the police don't think there will be. They believe she will be sold."

Brooke burst into tears, burying her head into Jon's shoulder and sobbing her heart out. "My baby, my poor, poor baby."

"Don't give up, darling. The police and FBI are on it, and there might be a way to get her back."

Brooke stopped crying and leaned back enough to see her husband's face.

"God has shown me some things, and it's important that I share them with you and ask you to walk with me through this. I'm not capable of doing this by myself. I need you, and I want you to be there. I want us to be strong and committed together."

Tears started to roll down her cheeks again. "That's been my prayer, Jon, for many months now. What can I do? Tell me what's going on."

"Come here." He sat down on the recliner and pulled her into his arms. She nestled there while he told her everything, everything he'd tried to deal with himself or hide from her. There were times he felt her trembling, but she didn't interrupt. As he revealed all that had happened and the decision they now had to make, he felt the tension slide away, and her unconditional love filled his heart.

"Brooke. I don't know what to do. Of course, I would give up the glasses in a moment if I thought it would save Amber, but then…"

"How can you trust what they promised you? Satan and his demons are liars. I understand. There's more at stake here. Do we trust God to save Amber, or do we deal with the devil?"

Jon loved his wife more than he could explain at this moment. She did understand. She knew the struggle.

"Jon, I wish I had the answer. I'm terrified for Amber. I don't know what you should do."

Together they slipped to their knees, and Jon led them in a prayer of humility and surrender.

"Please, God, show us what to do. Amen," Jon finished the prayer.

"Amen, Father."

"Amen," a soft voice echoed from the bed across the room.

The couple stood up and went to bed, where Brooke's mother looked at them with tired, beseeching eyes.

"You have to save my granddaughter." Her voice was still quiet but desperate.

"I'll find a way, mom," he assured her.

Jon had thought she was asleep when he gave the news to Brooke. Apparently, she wasn't, at least not the entire time. He wondered how much she had heard. Now he wished he had taken Brooke somewhere else to tell her. He hoped this wouldn't set back her mother's recovery.

Her mother's words brought Brooke's fear, rushing back even more potent. "Jon, I trust God, I do, but he gave us Amber. He trusted us with her life. Jon, look at me. Jon. You have to save Amber."

"I will. No matter what it takes."

****

Jon left the hospital after reassuring both his wife and his mother-in-law that he would find a way to get Amber back. As he walked through the hospital and headed for the parking lot, he looked like a man who had been beaten down. His mind at first was blank, too numb to have any thoughts at all, let alone a clear one. Getting into his car, he drove back home and went to his daughter's room, sitting down in front of her broken computer once more.

The screen still showed her emails, and he stared at them like a zombie until he realized that a new one had come in since the last time he had looked at the screen. Curious, his mind blinked back on like a rebooted computer. He clicked on the email, opening it up.

"Put on the glasses and look behind you."

The words, carefully crafted so that the two broken circles would not prevent him from reading the whole thing, sent chills up his spine.

Jon reached into his pocket and put the glasses on before gently spinning around in the chair to face the demon.

Slipknot stood before him. It's evil grin firmly affixed in place. "I've come for your decision."

"What choice do I have?" Jon asked brokenly. "I will do as you ask."

"Now, see? That wasn't so hard. You humans are so easy to manipulate. You each have your own special triggers. All we demons have to do is find them. So, how do you plan to get rid of them?"

"I don't know," Jon admitted.

"Well, think fast. Whatever way you do it, they must be gone for good. If you try to retrieve them in any way, we will destroy Amber. No matter where she is, we will be able to get to her and believe me. You won't like what will happen to her. And if that happens, we will make sure that it destroys your marriage as well. Brooke will hate you, and we will fuel that hate to the breaking point."

Slipknot's words should have told Jon that it couldn't be trusted, but he was so beaten down that he could no longer think straight. Even his training as a psychiatrist appeared to fail him. He could no longer pick up on the verbal and visual clues that normally helped him read a patient, or in this case, a demon. If nothing else, his faith in Brooke should have warned him, just as she had cautioned him. She was stronger in her faith than he was. He should have known that nothing could make her hate the way the demon suggested.

"So, how will you get rid of them?" The demon pushed. "Will you bury them? Throw them away? Break them into little pieces? Set them on fire? How?"

Slipknot's final suggestion triggered a response from Jon. Whatever he decided to do, he could not destroy them.

"No, I won't destroy them." *But maybe I should,* he thought. *If I destroyed them, no one would ever have to go through this torment again.*

"Be reasonable, Jon. The glasses have brought nothing but pain and suffering. The man who originally crafted them died in an asylum. His grandson killed himself. Then there's you. What you face is even worse – the destruction of those you love the most. Are the glasses really worth it?"

Are they? Jon thought about Paul and the words he had said. *This may be war, Paul, but it's one I can't win. The cost is too great.* Aloud he said, "I could put them in a bank box, but eventually someone would open it after my death. Then it could start all over again. My daughter wouldn't touch them, but her children might be curious and..." He shook his head, rejecting that idea. "I could bury them, but where? It would have to be someplace where no one would ever find them."

"Burial seems to be a good choice," the demon said. A sly grin crept on his deformed face.

"Of course, if I threw them in the trash, they would end up in a landfill somewhere. It's doubtful anyone would ever see them again."

"Better still," Slipknot said with a nod. "Either of those choices is good, so make up your mind and do it. Quick, before I change my mind."

There they were again – words that should have triggered a response in Jon, but they didn't.

"Fine. I'll bury them, but where?" Jon thought and thought until it finally came to him. "I know just the place."

Slipknot's grin continued to creep, a sign of his growing power.

"When will I get Amber back?" Jon asked as he looked up.

"In a day or two, once you've finished the job. It will take that long to set everything into motion," Slipknot told him.

"And how will you know that I've done what you asked?"

"I will stand there and watch you do it," the demon said with a grin.

"Then there's no time to waste."

Jon went to his office and turned on his own computer. He needed some information, and he had to be able to see it without the distortion of Amber's broken screen. Doing a search of the local newspaper's obituaries, he found the one about Carson and what cemetery he was buried in. Armed with that information, he planned to visit the caretaker in the morning to locate the exact grave, since it was too soon for it to have a grave marker yet.

****

The grass had grown over the gravesite already. A footer had been poured to set the marble stone, once the carving was finished. Exhausted from little sleep that had been filled with nightmares, Jon knelt and set down the briefcase he had brought with him. He felt like he needed to say a few words before doing what he had come to do.

"I'm sorry, Carson. I'm sorry you felt you had to end your torment by taking your life. I understand it, though. God knows that I do. I'm sorry I didn't believe you until I saw what you experienced with my own two eyes. What I don't understand is why the glasses came into being in the first place. It's not like your grandfather set out to create them on purpose."

Popping the latches on the case, he removed a small trowel and carefully lifted the sod and set it aside before digging deeper. Then he was down about six inches, he removed the glasses from the case. He had wrapped them in a washcloth and secured the ends together with masking tape. He wasn't sure why, except that for some reason, he did not want them to become scratched up from the dirt.

Laying them in the hole, he replaced just enough dirt to keep the sod from sticking up noticeably. The rest he scattered about the area so that it would eventually blend in. Then he placed the trowel back in the briefcase and closed it. Looking down at the grave once more, he finished what he had to say.

"I'm sorry about giving these back to you, Carson. Somehow, burying them in the sanctified ground seems like a sacrilege, but then the glasses aren't evil. Are they? It's what they reveal that is evil. Who knows? Maybe burying them with you will finally bring about the peace they destroyed. I hope so."

Jon stood up. He pressed his foot against the sod to make it secure. Then grabbing his briefcase, he walked away from the grave.

Slipknot rubbed his hands together and grinned at his leader. "Are you satisfied?"

Crump harrumphed. "I suppose it will do for now, as long as he stays away from them, and no one digs them up."

"He won't dig them up. He's too afraid of what will happen to his daughter if he does. As for anyone else, no one goes digging around in a gravesite."

Crump grinned wickedly. "So, what do we do with Amber?"

Chapter Twenty-Six

Just an Ordinary Day

Jon stood in line at the coffee shop just like he had so many times over the past few years, waiting to order two coffees and a Danish for Phil. Looking around, he watched the people the same way he had before his life had been turned upside down. He had given up. No glasses, no spiritual reality, ignorance was bliss. Life was more comfortable this way. *This isn't bad. Life is normal*, he thought. *I can be normal. Maybe this is why God doesn't want us to see them.*

Who was he trying to kid? He couldn't be carefree. Amber was missing. He looked around again, apprehensive, checking every nook and cranny. Were they there? Were they watching him? Not knowing made his chest muscles feel tight. Would he eventually get over this? Could they ever fade into the background again and let him return to what life was like before he had looked through the glasses? He doubted it. While he waited to order, he overheard a casual conversation.

"Here's the thing. She's totally in denial," the first woman said.

"You think?" her companion asked.

"Absolutely. She refuses to accept what is really happening. It's heartbreaking."

"Maybe it's better that way," the companion said, shaking her head sadly.

"Are you kidding? She shouldn't deny the truth. He's nothing but trouble. Otherwise, nothing will change. He'll continue to lie, and she'll believe him. It will go on and on, driving her into the ground until she's so beaten down, she won't be able to fight back."

"But what can she do?"

"Stop being a victim. Confront him," the first woman said vehemently. "Show him that she isn't going to stand by and let him ruin her life. Then she should toss him out. Put an end to it."

Jon let the women's words wash over him. He did not want to think about them. Their story sounded too much like his own. It reminded him of Paul's words and the need to fight back. That was different then. Amber's life wasn't on the line. To distract himself, he turned to the man behind him, a black police officer who had just gone off duty and was looking for something sweet and a shot of caffeine before heading home.

"Good morning, officer. Allow me to buy you a cup of coffee and whatever pastry you want."

The officer's eyebrows raised in surprise. "Why, thank you, sir. That's very kind of you."

He stepped up to the counter and ordered a coffee and a cinnamon roll, to which Jon added his two coffees and a Danish. The officer thanked him again and walked over a table in the corner to enjoy his breakfast.

Jon paid for the order and looked at the three monkeys: See no evil. Hear no evil. Speak no evil. *Words to live by,* he thought. If only he had followed their advice from the beginning. He approached the ladies he had overheard earlier as he headed for the door, saying with a smile. "Sometimes it's just better to leave things alone."

****

Jon walked down the street slowly. He was tired and felt like his energy had been sapped from him, making him move almost mechanically as he approached Phil at his regular spot. Phil had an old, worn Bible open that he was reading, holding it in his left hand, while the index finger of his right hand traced the passage he read. Jon handed him coffee. Phil thanked him and closed the Bible, stuffing it into a large front pocket of his cargo pants. He smiled as Jon started to hand him the pastry, but he didn't take it.

"Give that cheese Danish to Vivian. You know I only eat raspberry."

Surprised, Jon looked at the outside of the plain white bag, wondering how Phil knew that the pastry was cheese. He hadn't been paying attention and thought it was raspberry. Phil's next words caught him off guard.

"Do you think they are going to stop if you quit? They won't, you know."

"Who's quitting?" Jon dragged his thoughts away from the pastry and looked at Phil, puzzled.

Phil's expression was one of patience and understanding. "You're giving up."

"What are you talking about?"

"Hmmm. Really? Body language. It screams 'defeat.' You quit."

"Body language?" Jon asked sarcastically. Normally, this all might have made sense to him, but in his current funk, the words just flowed around him like a wayward wind.

Phil shrugged and then changed the subject. "Coffee's very good this morning. Must be a fresh pot. Needs a little more cream, though." He took a sip. "Ah, that's better."

It took a while, but the strangeness of the conversation finally penetrated Jon's numb brain. "Who are you?"

"You haven't figured it out yet? I'm your guy. You're my assignment. You know, everybody's got one, and I'm yours."

"You're my what? You're my…"

"Go ahead. Say it."

"Say what?"

Shaking his shoulders and looking at Phil's 'hump," Jon said, "You never cease to amaze and surprise me. My offer is still open. Any time you want to come talk to me. I'm available. Free of charge."

"I don't need your help, Jon. You need mine. Listen to me. Don't quit. Don't give up on Amber. Things aren't going to turn out the way they promised. You can't trust them. You can't believe a word they say. Their essence is nothing but lies and deception. If you give up now, Amber is lost."

"What do you know about Amber?"

"Amber needs your help. She needs you to fight. She needs her father to fix this."

Jon looked concerned, surveyed Phil again, and his hunchback. Then his phone rang. It was Brooke. Placing it to his ear, he said, "Hi, Hon. How are you doing? Just hang in there. Yes, of course.."

Jon turned to go into the office, and Phil called after him. "Oh, and Jon, tell Vivian that her mom missed her flight."

Jon looked back at Phil and walked inside the building, perplexed.

Phil raised his coffee cup and mouthed the words "to the battle."

In the lobby, a plane crash news story was splashed all over the TV screen. The scene of the wreckage was wide-spread and horrendous. Police, ambulances, and fire trucks were everywhere, bathing the devastation in red and blue light. Smoke and fire added yet another element of horror, making it feel surreal. Vivian stood in front of the TV in shock.

"My mom is on that plane. My mom… My mom is…is… Oh, Jon!" She broke down and began to cry in great shuddering sobs.

Jon took Vivian into his arms, patting her back and whispering useless platitudes to try and calm the heartbroken woman. He looked up at the TV screen, as Carl, one of Tom's patients, left, and he couldn't help thinking. *Did they do this? Did they influence someone to overlook or do something that sent this plane crashing to the ground?* He shook his head. Surely not. For the second time today, he almost wished he had the glasses back. If he did, what would he see?

Then Phil's words came back to him. "Uh, Vivian, I don't think your mom was on that plane."

"What?" She looked up at him, grief and bewilderment partially closing her reddened eyes. She was about to ask him to repeat what he had just said when her cell phone rang. She fumbled for it in her pocket, and when she brought it out, she nearly dropped it as her mother's face and phone number were showing as the caller. She answered it almost fearfully, thinking. *Is this a joke? Is this mom calling me from…beyond?* She mentally shook herself. "Hello?"

"Sweetie, It's mom. I just heard the news and wanted to call you right away so you wouldn't worry. I missed my flight. I wasn't on the plane. I'm okay."

Vivian let go of Jon. The play of emotions on her face ran the gamut. She began laughing and twirling around. "Mom! Oh, I was so …Oh, mom, it's so good to hear your voice. I can't believe it! Oh! Thank God!"

Once again, Phil's words echoed through Jon's head, this time making an impact. He ran out to find him, but Phil wasn't there. Seeing a boy on a bike riding by, he called out to him. "Hey, have you seen the homeless man who sits here every day?"

"What guy?" The boy shook his head and rode off.

Feeling more bewildered, Jon looked around and spotted the postman approaching his door. "Hey, did you see a guy leave here just a few minutes ago, you know, the one who hangs out here every day?"

The postman looked perplexed and shook his head no.

"You know who I mean - the guy who sits here…wears a green sports coat. Homeless guy, about 50. I bring him coffee every morning."

"Sorry, never seen him, and I have been working this route for the past ten years." The postman looked at the psychiatrist sign and back at Jon. "Are you a patient?"

"No, I'm the doct..." the end of the word drifted away as his cell alerted him to an incoming text. Amber's face and number were on screen. With shaking hands, he opened it. It read: "Daddy I'm..." The text stopped.

"No. No! Amber!" Frantically, he dialed her number, and it began to ring. *Come on. Come on. Amber. Answer the phone. If there's any way at all, pick it up, please.* But no one answered.

Jon looked down, fighting for control. Out of the corner of his eye, he spotted Phil's 0.99 cent notebook sticking out between the steps with a single white feather poking out of it. He opened the notebook to where the feather was resting and looked at the words printed neatly on that page. "Go see Paul. He will help you find Amber. "

Stuffing everything into his pocket, Jon ran back up the steps and poked his head through the doorway.

"Cancel my appointments for the rest of the day," he called out to Vivian before running back out and heading for the bookstore. He hoped Paul would have the answers he needed because he couldn't find Phil, whom he now realized was an angel. He also realized that he had been tricked.

Why did he leave? Where did he go? Just when he needed him the most. Just when he finally understood what Phil's words had meant all those mornings for so long. Now, no Phil, just a white feather from a wing and something else.

Chapter Twenty-Seven

Looking for Angels

Jon walked through the front door of the book store, looking for Paul.

"Paul! Are you here? Paul!"

"Back here, Jon."

Jon made a beeline to a shelf against the back wall where the store owner was putting a book back. "A lot has happened since you went on vacation."

"It wasn't a vacation. It was a speaking engagement."

"Speaking of which, don't you find it odd that when I needed you the most, you got called away to replace a speaker who suddenly took ill?"

Paul turned his face toward Jon and gave him an odd look. "Really?"

"Really."

When Paul did not say anything more, Jon continued. "Do you know someone named Phil?"

"I know a few someones named Phil," Paul replied

"This Phil says he's an angel."

"Ah, that Phil," Paul said knowingly.

"So you do know him?" Jon asked, trying to hold back his impatience.

"We've shared some coffee together."

"What can you tell me about him?"

"I can tell you that two months ago, he told me a man would come here who needed my help."

Jon nodded eagerly. "He also told *me* things that would happen, and they did, just like he said. I think he's an angel."

"Well, if you believe in that sort of thing," Paul responded with a small smile and a wink. "Let's go sit." Paul turned toward the center of the store and made his way over to the chairs by the fireplace. "I knew it was you Phil was talking about the first time you came here."

"You did? How?" Jon shook his head. "Never mind. Did he tell you about my daughter, Amber?"

"No, he just said you would need help in understanding the spiritual world. What about Amber?"

"I think I messed up. I'm not sure. You were gone, called away." He gave him an exasperated look when Paul did not respond. "Anyway, I didn't know what to do. One of the demons came to me."

"Go on."

"That doesn't surprise you?"

"No. Go on."

"My daughter has been abducted, kidnapped. Last night. She's being trafficked into slavery. The demon told me…showed me all this. He claimed he was responsible, and he made an offer – an offer to return my daughter unharmed if I did what he told me to do."

"What was it?"

"If I get rid of the glasses, never use them, and make sure no one else does, he'll return Amber to us unharmed."

"And?"

"What choice did I have, Paul? He orchestrated this whole thing. He even showed me where Amber was being held - right on her own computer screen." Jon stopped, overcome, as he fought back the tears. "There's no doubt about it. They, the demons, have her, and they were going to hurt her badly if I didn't do what they wanted." Jon stopped, expecting Paul to answer, but Paul just waited for him to continue.

"I got rid of the glasses. Immediately. They're gone. No one will ever find them."

Paul looked at him with compassion. "I'm sorry, Jon. I'm so sorry they are attacking your family and you. You must be a real threat to them."

Jon's mind was working overtime as he turned all this over. He looked at Paul, putting his thoughts into words. "Why would Phil send me to you and say that you would help me with Amber? Why, if I made this deal with the demon, would I need help from you? He promised to send Amber home safely. He promised, Paul. Answer me. Why?"

"I think you know why," Paul replied solemnly.

"He's not going to keep his word, is he?"

"According to the Bible, Satan is the father of lies. His demonic army follows in his footsteps. Can you honestly say that you expect him to keep his word?"

"They didn't want me to have the glasses. I thought it was a good trade."

"It might have been if they were telling the truth."

"I just want my daughter back and my old, normal way of life."

"If you are counting on the demons, I'm afraid you're not going to get either one of those things."

"They told me I would."

"Jon, they lie. That's what they do."

"Don't you think they want the glasses out of my hands bad enough to make the trade? She's just a young girl, what good is she to them?"

"She is fresh and innocent, the type of prey they love to hurt the most. And she is everything to you, and that's what makes her important. They're out to destroy you, your family, and everyone around you, your entire world if they can. Yes, they want the glasses destroyed so that they can never again be used against them, but they are tricksters, Jon. They will say and do anything necessary to get you to do what they want. Afterward, when it is too late, then you learn that everything they promised was a lie."

Jon's face changed suddenly as if he could see something beyond that room. "No matter what I do, they're not going to return Amber, are they? She's in just as much danger as she was before, more so now than ever. I am such a fool. Oh God! Forgive me for listening to their lies."

"God knows how clever the enemy is. He also has already forgiven you. Now, how will you respond to their plans?"

Jon looked around the bookstore, the expression on his face clearly revealing what his thoughts were.

"Don't worry. They're not here, Jon. We are protected."

"I'm going to retrieve the glasses. At least then I will know what they are planning. If I can hear and see them, then maybe I could find out where Amber is so that I can save her."

"Where are the glasses?" Paul asked.

"Buried in the cemetery. I put them in Carson's grave."

"Looks like we will need a shovel."

****

The two men drove to the cemetery and through the main entrance. Jon knew the exact spot he needed to find. The twists and turns that led to various parts of the graveyard were imprinted in his mind like a road map. He wished it was because it was Carson's grave, but it wasn't. It was the glasses and the curse that had been laid upon him and his family because of them and what they could do. When he reached the spot near the grave, he parked the car. He and Paul got out, and Jon walked around the back of the car to the trunk where he had stashed the shovel after burying the glasses that awful night.

This time though, it was broad daylight. It had been dark when he had buried them. As he slammed the lid of the trunk shut, he wondered about the correlation: By burying them, he had pitched himself into darkness. Would digging them up bring him back into the light?

Jon started to walk, but he stopped when he realized that Paul wasn't with him.

"Are you coming?" he asked, forgetting that Paul was blind.

"I can't see in the dark."

"It's not dark."

"For you. I'm not in my store. I have no frame of reference and no idea where to go, but I will come anyway. He pulled a briefcase out of the front seat. "Make-believe we are family mourners. Grab some flowers on the way in."

Jon looked around until he found a white plastic vase with red and white silk flowers and a large red bow. Pulling it out of the ground, he said to the person buried

197

there, "Sorry, I need to borrow these for a few minutes." Then with the shovel and flowers in one hand, he took Paul's elbow with his other hand and led the way through the cemetery until he found Carson's grave.

"It's here," he said, stopping and facing Paul toward the gravesite. After placing the flowers in front of the footer for the headstone, he began to carefully pull back the sod he had removed only a day ago and began to dig until a shout made him jump.

"Hey, you can't dig anything up," the groundskeeper shouted as he hurried over from where he had been working.

"Oh, we're not," Paul told him. "We're actually burying something next to my friend."

"Yeah? I don't know about that. What is it?" the groundskeeper asked.

Paul pulled a book out of his briefcase and held it up for the man to see. "This book. It was his favorite. See? It's even signed by the author."

While Paul distracted the groundskeeper, Jon deftly lifted the glasses out of the hole he had just dug and slipped them in his pocket.

"He wanted it buried with him, but with the tragedy of his passing and all, we forgot to put it in his casket at the service. I know it's too late to put it inside the casket, but we thought we should at least bury it in his gravesite, so we came to do it now." Paul slipped the book into the hole where the glasses had once been.

The groundskeeper was confused. "I guess it's okay."

"It was really stupid of us to forget, but it was one of his last wishes." Paul shook his head sadly. "If only we had known he was going to commit suicide when he asked us to bury this book with him, you know, for the next life. Maybe we could have done something to help him, to make him want to live."

"Oh yeah, I remember this guy." The man nodded understandingly. "Such a shame. What's the name of the book?"

"*Alive on the Other Side.*"

"Huh, maybe the book helped him make his decision." He looked at the spot where Jon had buried the book and replaced the sod. "Nice job. Well, you gentlemen have a good day," the groundskeeper said, wishing them well.

After he drove away in a golf cart, Jon pulled out the glasses, removed them from the cloth he had wrapped them in, cleaned them, and put them on. He looked around and commented with surprise. "I don't see any demons."

"Why would you? Nothing for them to do here. They believe that they have pulled the wool over your eyes and that you are too afraid to ever dig them up again."

They walked back to the car. Jon stopped to return the flowers that he had taken. He placed them back tenderly and said a small prayer of thanks.

****

Inside the car, Jon and Paul had to decide what to do next.

Jon checked his phone and saw that Tom had left a message two hours ago. He tried to call him back, but there was no answer. A chill went up to his spine. He thought about trying to find his friend, but then he knew what he had to do.

"To the Sanctuary?"

"Let's go see what they're up to."

Chapter Twenty-Eight

Sanctuary

Uncertain and terrified of discovery, Jon was about to enter the sanctuary with Paul. He knew what he had to do. At the same time, he was afraid of the demons discovering that he had dug up the glasses and was once again using them. Yet he knew that if he didn't do something, Amber would be lost to him. Taking a deep breath, he pulled back his shoulders and was about to step over the threshold when he felt a hand on his left shoulder. He nearly jumped out of his skin, because he knew it wasn't Paul. Paul was on his right. The hair on the back of his neck and arms stood up. Putting on the glasses, he turned and nearly fainted with relief. It was from Tom.

"Hey, sorry, Jon," Tom whispered. "I tried to call you."

"You nearly scared me to death," Jon whispered back. "What are you doing here?"

"Looking for Amber." Jon's puzzled look spurred him on. "No, I don't think she's here, but the demons might be."

"But you couldn't see or hear them," Jon replied. "What did you hope to accomplish?"

"I don't know!" Tom said exasperated. "I just knew I had to do something!"

Jon squeezed his arm and smiled gratefully. "Thanks, buddy. It means a lot that you have my back."

The three of them snuck inside, following Jon's lead. They moved slowly and as quietly as possible, ducking behind objects as they made their way toward the sanctuary. Fortunately, the demons were in chaos, too engrossed in their current business to even notice that they weren't alone. Jon whispered to the others, telling them what was going on.

"There are a host of demons here," he said. "They're really riled up. The reports coming in are about victories and defeats they have accomplished. The leader is standing there lording it over them, like the king of the universe." Jon peeked around and said to the others, "let's try and get closer."

As the three crouch-walked along the backside of a pew, Jon reminded them to be quiet, placing his index finger to his lips. Halfway down the row, they settled in, and Jon risked another peek over the pew. A demon turned, looked in his direction, and started walking toward them, sending a chill of fear up his spine.

"Get down," Jon whispered, warning the other two. "Crump is headed this way." The three crouched lower, paralyzed until Jon realized that the creature was just going to talk to a demon sitting a few pews in front of them.

"What is the update on this church?" Crump demanded as he approached.

Fotwhort left his seat and arrogantly walked up to the leader to give his report. "We have the pastor feeling very discouraged. He is beginning to think of this place as a business. We are working on some churchgoers as well, including the usual complainer, who is going to take issue with the whole church assembly about how the pastor's wife dresses. And that's just the beginning. They're going to pick her apart like vultures fighting over a piece of carrion."

"Very good."

"We also have most of the people believing their only commitment here is to attend church as spectators. They continue to be consumers and not contributors, which is perfect. One hour and they think they have done their service to Him for a week. Personally, I think it's brilliant that they call it a 'service.' That way, they think they've done their duty by sitting passively and enduring a whole forty minutes of spiritual talk."

Fotwhort laughed. "How little they know."

"Don't be coy," Crump said. "I heard that the worship leader is having an affair with one of the college girls."

"Not true. It's in the works, but it hasn't happened yet."

"Have her win a little in the lottery. Give her some cash and a little attitude," Crump suggested.

"Good idea. All right next." He turned to Slipknot, who had joined them during Fotwhort's report. "What's the latest on the counselor's daughter," Crump asked.

"Oh, everything's going as planned. She escaped, but she has been recaptured and secured. She is more terrified than ever!"

They all laughed.

"Shut up! This is a critical part of our plan," Crump growled. "The father is no fool. It took a personal appearance by 'yours truly' to convince him to give up the glasses in return for his daughter."

"But your Lordship, we have her where we want her. She's ours. You're not going to give her back, are you?" Slipknot asked.

"Idiot! Of course not."

"Your excellency, no one lies better than you! You're the master. Slipknot's as stupid as they come," Fotwhort said.

"Who are you calling stupid?" Slipknot demanded angrily.

202

"You! Why would you insult His Lordship?" Fotwhort asked. "The important thing is that he believed the lie. He thinks she is safe now and will be returned to him soon."

"Stupid human," Slipknot snorted.

The demons applauded.

The color drained from Jon's face. He turned around and sat on the floor, his back to the front. He now knew what Paul had tried to tell him.

"I was a fool," he whispered to Paul and Tom. "I placed my faith in God on the backburner and trusted instead in the lying deviousness of demons. Why did I do that?" He dropped his head into his hands.

"You were desperate and terrified about what would happen to your daughter," Tom said. "Anyone else in your shoes would have done the same thing."

"Paul wouldn't have," Jon replied, looking up at the blind bookstore owner.

"No, I wouldn't have," Paul agreed. "However, I have been fighting this battle for a lot longer than you have. I have had years to acquaint myself with the demon's ways and how they work. Don't give up on yourself, Jon. We'll find a way to save Amber."

Crump called over a new demon that had just popped into the room. The look on its face told him that trouble was ahead. "Report!"

Jon crawled out to listen to their conversation. Tom put a hand on his ankle and tried to stop him, but he couldn't. So, he waited with Paul.

"Sir, excuse me, sir," a quiet voice interrupted the revelry, "but it seems that the glasses that were buried are no longer there. I found an old book in their place."

Silence filled the room as everyone turned to their Leader, whose eyes appeared as smoldering red slits of rage and fury. Huge bat-like wings sprouted from his back, large curving horns sprouted from his head. Sharp, cruel fangs filled his mouth, presenting a visage so horrifying that Jon had to bite his lips and hold his breath to keep from gasping. He didn't move or speak, but Paul and Tom instinctively knew something terrible had happened as the room suddenly became unbearably hot.

"That contemptuous human worm! I know he is the one who went back for the glasses. No one else knew they were there. He has broken his vow to me! To me! Who does he think he is dealing with? A chump, a half-wit, an angel? Now, his daughter will suffer even more!"

Jon dropped to his knees, sweating, and crawled back to his friends. He whispered to Paul and Tom. "They know the glasses have been recovered. They know or think they know it was me. Either way, it doesn't matter. He, the leader, vows to make Amber suffer even more. Paul, I have to stop them!" The anguish on his face made Paul squeeze his shoulder in an effort to comfort him.

"Listen. Watch. We need more information," Paul warned him.

"But, the leader is so angry!" Jon whispered back.

"God isn't going to abandon us now. Just wait. Listen," Paul insisted.

Jon crawled forward again.

Crump turned to his subordinates, all of them cowering from his overwhelming anger. In his present form, he looked just like the most terrifying picture of Satan ever painted by a man. "You, you, and you," he pointed at three of his most cunning demons.

"Go and help our disciples with the daughter. See that she is taken care of so that her father knows exactly what she will experience."

"I have an idea," Slipknot said.

"What's your plan?" Fotwhort asked.

"I am going to send a special unit to help my 'disciple' with Jon's daughter." Slipknot grinned, rubbing his hands together. "You will be able to claim a double victory, oh great evil one."

"Good. I am looking forward to seeing the father crushed in defeat when they sell his daughter. Here is where she is."

Jon watched as the leader created a large, visual image of a broken down, filthy house. The number 654 was painted in black next to the screen door that was barely hanging on its hinges. The very thought of his daughter being in such a place made him shiver with revulsion.

"You know this place. We've used it before. It's on Twelfth Street. Our disciples are holding her and one other girl in the basement of this house. You know Francis, give him some new ideas, crueler than usual. I want to finish this battle with a flourish!" Crump shouted.

Jon crawled back and crouched next to his friends. Tom gave him a sympathetic look.

"They have her in the basement of a house at 654 12th Street. They are going to really hurt her if we can't stop them. We have to go - now!"

As the three crept across the floor toward the side exit, Jon heard the leader give one more command.

"And find Jon, that double-crossing slime. Stop him. Whatever he's up to, stop him."

"Where is he now?" Fotwhort asked.

"Our last report was that he was at the bookstore," Slipknot said.

"No!" Crump's wings raised up, darkening the room and making the demons around him pull back even further. "I don't want him or anyone else around that man. He is not good for our cause."

Jon heard those words just before they left the church. They ran to his car. Upon arrival, he turned to Paul. "Why are the demons so afraid of you?"

"Afraid? No, I don't believe afraid is the correct word," Paul replied. "They hate me and are leery of me."

"Why?" Jon repeated.

"Because I have been a stumbling block for them for many years now."

"So that's why Phil send me to you," Jon said.

"In part, but also as a means to help educate you about the battle and as a way to provide you with the weapons you would need."

Tom looked from one to the other. "Who's Phil? Wait! Phil? The homeless guy that sits outside the office every day waiting for the coffee and Danish you bring him? That Phil?"

"That Phil," Jon replied.

"Why would a homeless man send you to Paul? How does he even know Paul?"

"Because he is an angel," Jon replied.

Tom looked from Jon to Paul and back. Apparently, Paul believed the same because he did not disagree. "Well, where is he then? He should be right here helping." He looked from man to man. "Right?"

"The men that have Amber are evil, but they are not demons, only influenced by them," Paul said.

"Should we call the police then?" Tom asked.

"Yes," Jon replied. "They can meet us there."

Chapter Twenty-Nine

In Pursuit

The three men hurried out of the sanctuary, talking quietly as they ran.

"We don't have much time," Jon said. "The demons are very angry that I dug up the glasses. They'll be pushing their minions to hurry up and do whatever it is they have planned for the girls."

"If they are planning on selling the girls into slavery, they may not be able to move as quickly as the demons want," Paul offered encouragingly. "These things don't just happen out of the blue. If that were the case, the girls would be out of our reach already."

"I hope you're right," Jon replied.

As Jon ran ahead to get the car, Tom helped Paul through the church and outside to the parking lot, making sure the blind man did not stumble over or run into anything. Because he could not see or hear the demons, Tom had the creeps. He kept looking over his shoulder to see if they had been discovered, even though he couldn't have seen them anyway.

"It's okay, Tom," Paul said, trying to reassure him. "They haven't discovered us yet."

Jon drove his car up to the door of the church, and Tom helped Paul find the back door and get inside. Then he climbed into the front seat with Jon, who was on his cell with his wife.

"So, that's the gist of what's happening. We are on our way to the address given by the demon. That's where Amber and this other little girl are being held. I've also phoned the police, and they are on their way as well. Keep praying for us and for the safety of the girls. I have no idea what is going to happen, but one way or another, we're going to rescue them if it's the last thing we do."

"Be careful, Jon," Brooke urged him. "You don't know what kind of people they are. I mean, we know they are horrible people, but they may have guns. I want to get Amber back and rescue the other girl, but I don't want to lose you in the process."

"I'll be careful, Brooke. Promise. Remember, the police will be there, too, and they have guns and will protect us. I've got to go now and concentrate on my driving."

"Good luck! I love you," she said, fighting to keep the tears from her voice.

"I love you, too."

When everyone was belted in, Jon drove away from the church. He wanted to drive as fast as he could, but he realized that it would not be wise to do so. The last thing he needed was to get into a wreck or to be pulled over for speeding. Chances are, the officer would never believe his story, and he could end up in jail again, instead of on his way to rescue Amber.

Now that Tom believed what Jon had been saying all this time, he found that he had some questions. Questions that he hoped Paul would have the answers to. He turned around in his seat to look at the man he was just learning played an important part in this whole nightmare scenario. "Why would God allow this to happen?"

"We live in troubled times, where Satan, the fallen angel, and his demons were thrown when he rebelled against God. And because humans have been given free will, it also gives him the power to wreak havoc on the world."

"That doesn't seem right. Why should we have to suffer because of Satan's disobedience?" Tom asked.

"I suppose that's one way to look at it. I'm sure that wasn't God's intention."

"Then why doesn't He just deal with the devil and put an end to it?"

"I'm afraid only God knows the answer to that question. There will be a time and place for the reckoning, until then, we must fight the battles we are faced with and try to stop as much evil as we can, but evil is powerful."

"How much power does the devil have?" Tom asked.

"He influences humans in every way he can. The more influence or control he has, the more evil he creates."

"But what about God's influence?"

"God is more powerful, and he will defeat Satan when our time on the earth ends. There's really no contest. In the meantime, Satan wants to influence and take as many souls with him to eternal damnation as he can before God intervenes."

"So, there is a constant battle for people going on between them, and all because of free will. I wonder if we wouldn't be better off without it," Tom said, turning back around in his seat.

The words had barely left his mouth when out from the left side of the road, a huge male deer suddenly leaped into the road and crashed into the car. The buck was thrown up on top of the hood, spinning the car around until it came to a stop. As the heavy animal landed, its head cracked the windshield, and one of its antlers penetrated the window, stopping an inch from Tom's face.

Tom jerked his head back in shock. He was shaken to the core.

"Is everyone okay?" Jon asked, looking from Tom to Paul and then back to Tom. Seeing how close his friend had come to serious injury, shook him up as well.

In the back seat, Paul bowed his head and prayed. "Lord, thank you. Thank you for your protection."

Tom threw Jon an incredulous look at Jon. "Is he crazy?" he asked, referring to Paul. "I was inches from being killed. One inch, actually."

"What happened?" Paul asked, making Tom feel a bit guilty. He had forgotten about the book seller's blindness.

"A deer tried to jump through our windshield," Jon responded.

"But, everyone's all right?" Paul asked.

"Yes. Yes," Jon assured him.

"Then, God protected us." The statement was so sure and final that it sent Tom into a tizzy again.

"Jumpin' Jehoshaphat! Would you look at that!" Tom exclaimed before turning to Paul. "Oh, sorry. There's a huge dead deer stuck in the windshield. I guess the enemy's getting creative. That was close!"

Jon had to know. Pulling out the glasses, he put them on and looked around, but he didn't see anything. If that deer had been propelled by the influence of a demon, it hadn't stuck around to gloat. Still, he didn't think this was mere coincidence. The demon leader wanted him punished, possibly even dead. One of his minions might have already looked for him at the bookstore. When he discovered that Jon wasn't there, he had sent others out to determine his location.

"Amber!"

"What is it?" Paul asked. "Do you see her?"

"No," Jon replied. "We have to get to her. I can't let this stop me from saving her!"

The men piled out of the car and gathered around the front.

"We have to get this thing off the hood so we can get going again," Jon said.

"But the deer's antler is stuck in the windshield," Tom said. "How are we going to get it out?"

"Let's try pulling it out," Jon suggested.

Tom guided Paul to the deer's front legs, while he took them back, and Jon grabbed hold of the head. They tugged with all their might, but the deer appeared to be stuck, it's antler hanging up on a vent in the dashboard and the cracked glass.

Looking around, Jon spotted a large rock along the side of the road. Retrieving it, he used it to smash out the rest of the window and clear out the glass, then tossing it aside, he climbed inside the car, pulled the antler out of the vent, and shoved the deer's head, until it cleared the dashboard. Leaving the car, the three of them tugged and pulled until the animal finally slid off the car to the side of the road.

Then Jon surveyed the damage. What he saw made him visibly upset. "It will take a miracle for this car to run now."

The front end was smashed in, the hood severely indented so that it looked like someone had tried to mold it to the interior parts underneath it. Still, they all got back into the car. They just couldn't give up now. Turning the key, Jon tried to start the car. It gave a couple of weak groans and then stopped. Jon tried again and again without success.

"God, we would appreciate it if you would start this car and make it drivable," Paul prayed. "Satan's trying to stop us from reaching Amber and saving her. Please, Lord, amen." He turned toward Jon. "Try it again."

If it hadn't been for urgency, Jon felt in trying to rescue his daughter, he might have given up. Each time he had tried, it sounded like the battery was getting weaker. Then he remembered what the demons had said about Paul. He thought about the angel, Phil, or whatever his name really was, who seemed to believe that the bookstore owner had some extraordinary power or possible 'in' with God. Maybe, just maybe if he believed…. He turned the key once more, and the car roared to life.

Tom and Jon exchanged looks of surprise, a wow expression on their faces.

The car appeared to be totally undrivable, and Jon had to compensate for its quirky slant and other damage. He looked at the clock on the dashboard. It had also been smashed by the antler and no longer worked. Glancing at his watch, he saw that the delay had cost them ten precious minutes. Had the police arrived yet? Were they waiting for him? Or would they go ahead and break down the door.

No, this would be a hostage situation, he thought. *They might try to negotiate first, but what if that failed? What if the kidnappers were able to sneak the girls out unseen, while one of them stayed behind to do the so-called negotiating? What if….* Jon had to force his mind to shut out all the what-ifs and concentrate on trying to drive his wrecked car.

As he urged the car forward as fast as he dared, clanging and banging noises emerged from under the hood. Then he thought he heard a slight hiss.

"Is that the radiator?" he asked.

"If it is, the car will start to overheat," Tom replied. "Keep an eye on your temperature gauge.

While Jon continued driving on a wing and a prayer, he couldn't help wondering, *Where is God in this story, and why would He allow this to happen? Don't get me wrong,* he continued, turning his thoughts to God. *I am grateful that You are somehow making this car run, but that deer running into us has cost us valuable time, time that Amber might not have.*

He would later discover that the delay allowed the police to arrive on the scene first. If they had been the first to get there, things might have gone very wrong.

"All things work together for good to them that love God. Romans 8:28," Paul said.

His words sent a chill down Jon's spine. "How did you know what I was thinking?" He glanced into his rearview mirror.

Paul nodded knowingly but said nothing.

The car limped along for another five miles until a police car pulled them over, the officers thinking that obviously, this car shouldn't be running. Jon threw up his hands and pulled over, frustrated by yet another delay.

When the policeman approached the driver's window, Jon rolled it down.

"How are you driving this wreck?" the officer asked.

He explained the situation, and the look he received from the cop was incredulous.

"Please, just check with the station, or the kidnapping bureau, or whatever. They'll confirm our story. And please hurry. I've got to rescue my daughter."

The officer shook his head, but when he looked into the back and saw Paul, something in the man's expression made him call it in. This story was almost too fantastic to be made up.

It seemed to those in the car that it took forever, but the officer finally got the okay to let them go.

"Okay, your story checks out. So, I'm going to escort you to the scene. What is the address?"

Jon gave him the information. Crossing his fingers, he turned the key, and the wrecked car somehow was able to start again, even though it was really messed up. This was beyond reason or understanding.

"How on earth is this thing still running?" the officer asked.

"Holy Spirit fuel injection," Paul responded.

The officer shook his head as he headed back to his vehicle. "I have to get me some of that," he said under his breath.

The police car started off, running silent, but with its lights flashing, leading the way.

Paul continued praying in the back seat, "Lord, please keep this car running."

As if in answer, the car jumped ahead, catching up to the police unit, and easily keeping pace. When the officer checked his rearview mirror, he was amazed to find them right on his tail.

"Holy Spirit fuel injection. Huh."

* * *

Chapter Thirty

The House

When Jon, Tom, and Paul arrived at the kidnappers' house, numerous police and FBI vehicles lined the street, although none of them had lights or sirens going. Further down on both ends of the street, the intersections were blocked off by additional police cars. Their lights flashing to keep traffic and bystanders away from the danger zone.

Lead Detective Fred Behnken stood on the sidewalk, two houses over, talking with the lead FBI agent, planning their approach.

"It looks like the suspects are inside," Detective Behnken said. "My men surveilled the house, and from what they could make out, there are lights on in the living room, and one over what we assume is the kitchen sink."

"How many people are inside?" The FBI agent asked.

"It's hard to say. The blinds on the windows are all closed. Probably to keep anyone from seeing the girls and what is going on inside."

"Are you sure this is the right house?"

"Yes, the address came from a trusted source, but that's not all. When my men examined the exterior of the home, they discovered a basement window with the words, 'Help, Kidnap,' and 'Basement,' scratched in the paint that someone had used to black it out. This is the place all right," Detective Behnken assured him. "We ran a search on the property, too. It belongs to Francis and Anita Navarro."

"Two women?"

"No, the man's name is Francis. He has a record as long as my arm, including assault, drunk and disorderly, and robbery, for which he served time. He was also brought in once on suspected kidnapping. However, the victim escaped and was too frightened to press charges or even testify. Nothing on the woman, but it appears that while in prison, he got chummy with a cellmate named Alan Greenbrier, a drug dealer and real nasty piece of work. If he's in on this, and I'll bet my next paycheck that he is, the girls are in real danger."

One of the officers approached the pair.

"What is it, Howie?" Detective Behnken asked.

"Something's up. There is a lot of noise going on inside. Sounds like two men arguing," the officer replied.

"Time to move in," the FBI agent in charge said.

Behnken agreed, and they had the swat team circle the house and get into position, ready to bust down both the front and back doors.

Seeing the action, Jon and the others, who were being held back by the policemen that had escorted them to the scene, took a step forward.

"What's happening?" Jon asked. "Are they going to bust in there? What if the kidnappers have guns? What if they use the girls as shields. They could be killed. They could..."

"Easy Jon," Paul said, laying a hand on his arm. "The police know what they are doing, and God will be there to guide them."

"Sorry, Dr. Rickner, but you need to stay behind me for your own safety," one of the officers said.

"But Amber is in there. I have to save her," Jon insisted.

"You have to stay back and let them do their job. You go running up there now, you will get in the way and jeopardize the operation. You could even get yourself or your daughter killed. Is that what you want?" the other officer asked.

Jon exhaled a shaky breath. "No. Of course not."

"Look, I know this is hard," Tom said, intervening, "but the police have done this kind of thing before. They know what they are doing. Just hang in there, buddy."

"Lord, please be with the officers as they attempt to rescue the girls. Keep them and the girls safe from harm, and help them capture these evil people," Paul prayed.

The officer, who had commented earlier on the spiritual fuel injection said, "If He answers your prayer like he did with that junker, everything will work out just fine."

Several men stood by the doors, while others covered the windows. They had been forewarned about the nature of the men inside, and they were determined not to allow them to escape. Ramming tools were brought to each door. Everyone remained quiet as they waited for the signal through an earpiece in their right ears.

The signal came.

BAM! BAM! BAM!

Sounded the twin echo as the front and back doors were bashed in. Police and FBI rushed into the house shouting.

"FBI!"

"POLICE!"

"Drop your weapons and drop to the floor!"

The men and women flowed through the rooms like an invading army. As others opened the basement door, switched on the light, and headed downstairs after getting no response to the shouts.

Calls resounded throughout, as the all-clear echoed from room to room.

Outside Jon was more afraid than ever for his daughter. His body shook with frustrated inaction as he looked out at the rundown houses in the neighborhood with dirt yards and junky old cars parked in the front yard. Even from his position, two houses away, he could hear the shouts and heavy footsteps of the police as they went through and cleared the house.

Inside, the police came upstairs from the basement.

"Did you find them?" The FBI agent in charge asked.

"They're gone," Detective Angie Morehouse replied. She had been one of the officers to go downstairs, believing that the girls would respond better to a woman. She felt sick over missing them and was deeply worried about them. "We found two chairs that they were duct-taped to, and some empty drink cups and partially eaten food. They were there, but where are they now?"

"Where indeed?" The agent said, turning to the only person in the house who wasn't law enforcement.

"What did you do with the girls? Where is your husband and Alan Greenbriar? Where did they take them? Answer me, damn it!"

"No hablo inglés!" Anita babbled, terrified by what was happening.

Like everyone else, the agent was frustrated and angry. The girls and the suspects were gone.

"Get somebody in here who speaks Spanish!" The agent yelled.

His continued yelling frightened Anita even more, and she cowered in the chair where she sat, looking even smaller than she was with her hands raised in the air.

Detective Morehead ran out of the house. "I need someone who speaks Spanish!" She shouted.

"I do," Tom shouted. "I can help."

Turning, she saw him, Jon, and Paul, who had broken away from the other officers and were running toward her.

"Let them come," she said to the officers, lifting up the yellow police tape to allow them through.

As other agents and officers filed out, leaving the scene for the CSI personnel now arriving on the scene, Jon felt his heart sink.

"Where's Amber and the other girl?" He asked.

"I'm sorry, Jon. They've been taken elsewhere."

Jon's knees felt weak, and he stumbled. Paul, who was hanging onto him as a guide, grabbed and steadied him.

"Hold on, Jon. They'll find them. Don't give up. Have faith."

Detective Morehead led them into the living room, where the FBI agent was still towering over Anita like a vengeful giant.

"Let me try," she told him. "She's terrified." When the agent gave her a look, she said, "I know. I know, but you aren't going to get anywhere bullying her, and if we're to find out what they did with the girls, we need to know as quickly as possible."

Heaving a sigh of disgust, the agent walked away to confer with someone else.

Turning to Tom, Morehouse said, "Tell her who Jon is. By the look of her, I'm not sure she knows the full extent of what her husband and the other man were doing."

Tom knelt in front of the woman and took her hands, talking soothingly to her as he tried to calm her down. Then he introduced Jon and told her who he was. Anita looked up at Jon, her eyes worried and apologetic at the same time. She spoke rapidly.

"She said that she knows her husband has changed and is doing something bad with the girls. Ever since he teamed up with his former cellmate, Alan Greenbriar, he has become a different man," Tom translated. "She said that Alan is crazy and a mean one, who threatened to kill her if she didn't do what he told her to do."

Anita spoke some more.

"She said that because she understands very little English, she thought they were just using the girls for ransom and that parents would get them back."

"Tell her that the men plan to sell the girls into sex slavery," Detective Morehouse said.

Tom did, and a torrent of words poured from her mouth. Now that she knew what the men were really up to, she fought back her fear and decided to cooperate with the authorities and help the girls as best she could. She told them about a warehouse, where she believed they were taken, and to look in the top drawer of the end table, where they found a scrap of paper that had the location scrawled on it.

Detective Behnken, who had joined them during the conversation, said, "I recognize that area. Let me check my tablet to see if there's a connection." Moments later, he looked up at them, saying, "there is. We've also discovered who the other kidnapped girl is. She's been missing for almost as long as Amber." He showed them her picture on his tablet.

"When you find Amm-ber and Brit-Ah-nee, tell them Ah-nee-ta sent help," Anita said in broken English. "Tell them God tells Ah-nee-ta to help." She crossed herself and prayed in Spanish for forgiveness for her husband, as she was put in handcuffs and led out of the house.

While the others made ready to converge on the new location, Detective Morehouse, who was a believer and understood, prayed together with Jon and the others for Amber and Britany's safety, and for God to protect them until they could get to them.

"Let's go."

They headed for the warehouse. Leaving the wrecked car behind, Jon, Tom, and Paul piled into Detective Morehouse's vehicle. They would later have to have it towed as it had done its job and would no longer start.

"The girls haven't given up, and neither should you," Morehouse said. "One of them, and I think it must have been Amber as the window is too high for the other girl to reach, scrawled help on the basement window."

Jon broke into tears.

"Remember, these guys don't know they are being influenced by the demonic, they are just doing what they think is for their own interests and benefits," Paul told Jon and Tom.

Jon nodded as he wiped his eyes and regained enough control to call his wife and inform her about what has gone down.

"Hang in there, Jon," she said encouragingly. "A small group of friends and family are here praying with me. God is going to save Amber and that other little girl, too. I just know it."

Chapter Thirty-One

At Last

Within moments of the FBI agent's order, six police and FBI cars and an armed hostage unit headed toward the warehouse district. Jon, Tom, and Paul rode with Detective Morehouse.

"The perp's wife gave us one address, but then corrected herself and gave us another, four blocks to the south. Three of the cars, under the direction of the FBI special agent in charge, will go to the first address. We'll follow the other three cars and the hostage unit to the second address," she explained as they raced through the town.

As they approached the warehouse district, they silenced the sirens and turned off their lights. Then splitting up, they cautiously approached the two addresses. Their microphones on, they parked at the back of the areas and silently exited their patrol cars.

At location number two, lead detective Fred Behnken walked over to Detective Angie Morehouse's car and told Jon and his friends to stay put.

"Any interference on your part could blow this whole operation, even cost the girls their lives. I don't know about Francis, but Alan is unstable, a veritable powder keg that could explode at any time, so please, listen this time and stay put until we give the all-clear."

The three men nodded.

"Don't worry, officer, we'll stay put," Tom assured him.

The hostage unit got into position, as the agents and officers, led by Detective Behnken, crept on foot up to the warehouse door.

"The girls are our number one priority. If you see them, get them out and to safety as quickly as possible."

The men and women nodded. They knew what to do. They entered precisely as they'd been trained, and within seconds had fanned out and were in position and ready.

"This is Detective Fred Behnken of the Boston Police Department," he called out. "We have the building surrounded. Send the girls out to us, and then come out with your hands up. Slide your weapons across the floor toward us, so we can see them. Every window and doorway is covered. You cannot escape. If you step out now and do as you are told, you won't be harmed."

His words were met with complete silence.

Behnken tried again, this time, when he called out, he addressed the perps by name. "Francis, Alan, we know you're in here. Send the girls out unharmed, and then we can talk. Do yourselves a favor. It's over."

The silence was so complete, Fred felt like he could have heard a mouse walk across the floor.

"Come on out, and we can talk. If you haven't harmed the girls, things will go much easier on you. Don't make us come looking for you. Be smart and don't make this any harder on anyone than it needs to be."

Silence again.

Using hand signals, Behnken sent the officers and agents in different directions to search the building. The detective kept talking, addressing only Francis this time, but to no avail. Within minutes, each of the officers returned empty handed - no girls, no bad guys, nothing. The warehouse was empty.

There wasn't a single person inside or outside the building. Although it appeared that someone had been there recently. They saw scuff marks in the dust and dirt on the floor, the kind that might be made by someone struggling to get away. But there was no clear-cut proof. It could have been anyone. The detective sent the men in again, guns were still drawn, but with flashlights. The look on his face was grim.

"Check everywhere, just in case the girls might have been stashed here."

"Should we look for bodies?" Detective Morehead asked solemnly.

Fred sighed heavily. "Yes. I hope we don't find any, but if they realize that we are onto them, they might have decided to take a loss and stash the bodies."

"I pray you are wrong."

"So do I."

As the officers spread out, Agent Behnken contacted the agent in charge of the other team at the first location. "Any luck?"

"Just a receptionist and two salespeople at this location. They sell computer components and software. Been here for five years. Nothing. We searched the whole place. They claim they haven't seen anything unusual in the area."

The detective sighed and turned to see Jon standing behind him. "I told you to stay in the car."

"Paul and Tom are still there. I had to be here. I stayed out of the way until I saw your men start coming out of the building. What if you had found her? I wanted her to know I was here. I wanted her to see me."

"There's no one in the building, Jon. The team's searched everywhere."

"Can I go in?" Jon asked, "I feel like she's been here."

"Sure. Come on." The detective led him inside the huge warehouse. It was dark and damp. Behnken's powerful flashlight lit up most of the area. "I sent the team in twice. If they were here, they're gone now. There's no one here."

"I don't know, it just seems like…it's just a feeling."

"The best thing we can do is go back to the station and question Francis's wife more thoroughly, especially after this turned up nothing. It seems she was only pretending to be helpful."

They walked outside and the detective called in his people. "Thank you, ladies and gentlemen. Let's get back to the station. I'm going to have some hard questions for that woman. Units one and two, stick with me. The rest of you can check-in, but be available if we get a break."

As Jon stood outside and looked at the beat-up warehouse, Tom approached him.

"Hey, how long has it been since you talked to Brooke?"

"Probably too long."

"Give her a call."

"Yeah, I will."

"Jon, we gotta leave," the detective called from her car.

"I'm going to stay here awhile, Angie." He turned to Tom. "You guys go. You have no idea how much I appreciate you, both of you. I can't say enough. Go, but don't stop praying."

"We've got you there, buddy," Paul replied.

"I know Amber was here. I…I just feel like I need to stay for a while, for some reason. Maybe I'll discover something."

"Are you sure?" Tom asked.

"Yes."

"All right. Hey, I'll take care of the car. Get it towed…and you know, whatever."

"Thanks, I forgot about that."

Detective Phillips pulled her car up next to the two and spoke to Jon. "Either Fred or I will call you as soon as we get some answers, or have any leads. I'll send another officer back to pick you up. How much time do you want here?"

"Give me a half-hour, forty-five minutes, unless something breaks, then call me."

The detective gave Jon her flashlight. "All right. Let's go, everyone."

Tom gave Jon a bearhug. Paul squeezed his shoulder and offered encouragement. "Listen to God, then go where He leads. You have the armor. Use it."

He and Tom got into the cruiser.

Jon watched them disappear, along with the other units. Then he turned toward the warehouse and flipped on the flashlight, walking to the middle of the room, where he got down on his knees.

"God, I'm desperate. I don't know what to do, where to go. I want to trust you to protect Amber, but it's hard. I want to believe you have control, but it doesn't feel like it. Do whatever you want with me, but please help me find Amber. You alone can save my daughter. I ask you this because I'm your child, and your son died for me. In his name, I'm asking you, please. Amen."

Jon stood and turned with his flashlight hitting each wall in the warehouse with its powerful beam. "Amber, I feel like you're here. Amber! Can you hear me? Make some kind of noise, sweetheart. I'm not leaving, Amber."

228

Jon's flashlight flickered and went out. He shook it, tried turning it on, banged it with his other hand. When he heard a laugh, he looked up. Crump, the head demon, the same one he'd met in Amber's room, stood there with a grin, illuminated by soft light from nowhere. He started walking around Jon in a circle. Suddenly there was another light, a spotlight in Jon's eyes. He raised his hand to block the light, and it dimmed slightly.

"You didn't keep your word, Jon. You said you would get rid of those glasses for good. Remember? That was our deal." The demon stopped and his dark, hollow eyes pierced Jon's. "Our trade, Jon. Amber for the glasses. The glasses for Amber."

Jon didn't say a word. He just looked at the ominous figure and prayed silently. "God, forgive my doubt. In the name of Jesus, give me the right response, the right words to defeat this creature, this enemy of yours. Help me put on your armor. "

"*You*," the demon bellowed with rage. "*You* broke your word. *You* lied. *You* will be responsible for Amber's death. You, Jon, *you*!" He paused and scanned the room with his eyes. "Do you hear that, Amber? It was your father who lied, who put his own desires before your life. *Your* father! He's the one who betrayed you, Amber. *Your* father!"

Jon stopped breathing and continued to pray. "God, give me strength, give me power. This is your battle."

"Oh yes, Jon. She's here. Amber is right in this building. I made sure she couldn't talk, or move, or make noises, and I cloaked her in darkness so that the others couldn't find her. Can you imagine her anguish? Her little heart beating so fast, when the police didn't find her - when you didn't find her?"

Two, then three, then a dozen demons joined Crump, laughing.

The horrible creature spread his arms to welcome the others and joined them in laughter. "She had hope, such hope. She thought her father was here to save her! Ha! Ha! Ha! Ha!"

Jon turned toward the demon. "For there is no truth in the devil. When he lies, he speaks his native language, for he is a liar and the father of lies."

Now a dozen other creatures appeared, angry. "You will not mock our lord!"

Jon stepped back for a moment in surprise. He closed his eyes, "Father God, help!" *I cannot face them alone,* he added silently.

Suddenly, Phil appeared beside Jon, not in his homeless clothing, but as a Commander of a legion on angels. Jon, however, was completely unaware of his presence. Then a group of warrior angels standing tall and powerful appeared behind Jon and Phil. They were silent, their swords at their sides, spears upright in their hands.

Jon quoted another scripture. "He unleashed against them his hot anger, his wrath, indignation, and hostility— a band of destroying angels."

There is a pause, some twitching, uncomfortable glances at one another as the creatures seem to be disoriented by the scripture and God's angels.

Then recovering, the lead demon shouted, "No, Jon, you are the liar. You're the one who broke your promise."

More demons joined the group. They appeared angry but uneasy and confused. These were the same demons that had been in the sanctuary.

More of God's Angel Army joined the others, more powerful, totally confident.

"The God of peace will soon crush Satan under your feet," Jon replied, his confidence climbing as he watched the demon cringe.

"Stop! Those words mean nothing!" Crump croaked.

"Since we have now been justified by Christ's blood, how much more shall we be saved from God's wrath through him!"

Now the demons were upset, snarling, but cowering. More angels appeared and took a step forward.

His voice quavering, the evil spirit fought for control. "Stop. I said, *stop!*"

"You are nothing but Satan's spawn, and God's enemy." Jon pointed his finger at the decrepit, ugly form. "You have already been defeated, Evil One. At the cross, Jesus defeated you and your corrupt lord, Satan. You may control some, but you will not control me. Jesus is my Lord. God is my Father. What, who, and how you attack me will have no bearing on my commitment to Him, the true God of the Universe!"

God's angels drew their swords, and now they surrounded Jon and Phil. The demons' eyes fixated on the angel warriors, and they began to shake, whether, in fear or rage, Jon didn't care.

"Amber is my daughter, and I love her, yes! Beyond words. But Jesus is my Lord, and He controls everything - in this world, and the world to come. You, however, have just a short time to boast and berate, to insult and attack God's people."

"You...you think?" The dark figure whimpered.

"*No!* I don't think. I *know!*" This time it was Jon who filled the room with his voice. "And you are done! You and your kind, along with your evil lord, will suffer forever. Amber and I, my family, we may suffer for a short time. You may cause injury and pain temporarily, but my Lord, my Savior, my God beats you every time! So, get out. Leave me. Leave my daughter. In the name of Jesus and because of his blood, I reject you and banish you from my presence. There is no name above His name. There is no power above His power and in that power, I claim deliverance from your evil! Now go!"

The light was gone. The demons disappeared. Jon stood, courageous and confident in the Holy Spirit.

God had kept His word.

Jon turned around as if feeling something and looked. The angels smiled at him as they sheathed their swords, but he did not see them.

"Good work, Jon," Phil whispered.

Jon turned toward Phil. He did not see him, but a fresh breeze touched his face, and the angels and Phil disappeared.

"Daddy. Daddy" It was Amber's voice. "Daddy, I'm here, under the floor."

Jon took off the glasses and stuffed them in his shirt pocket. Then the flashlight came back on, and he ran toward her voice in the corner of the room. A slit in the floorboards revealed a trapdoor. With tears of thanksgiving, he yanked it open, and there was Amber. Safe. He had found her!

Tears streamed down Jon's face as he reached for her.

"Daddy, this is Brittany."

Looking away from Amber, he realized another terrified, weeping girl sat tied up next to his daughter.

"Brittany. It's all right. You're both…you're both going to be all right," he assured them.

With a strength he never knew he possessed, Jon pulled his daughter out with one movement and embraced her with tears of joy.

"Daddy, oh daddy, thank you," she sobbed into his chest, then she pulled away. "Daddy, help Brittany."

Jon reached down again, and as he pulled the other younger girl out, the glasses slipped from his shirt pocket and fell into a dark corner of the hole.

He quickly untied them, observing their bruises and scrapes, his heart broke, and yet it was filled with thanksgiving.

"Daddy, who were you talking to?"

"I'll tell you all about it later. Let's go home."

With his arms around both girls, he walked them toward the light of the afternoon sun and freedom.

Chapter Thirty-Two

Resolution

Jon left the warehouse with Amber and Brittany, but without even a single thought for the glasses. He unknowingly had lost them while rescuing the girls, but he didn't notice it until he was outside with them. After checking his pockets, he turned to Amber and said, "I've got to go back inside for a minute."

"No, daddy, don't leave us out here alone," Amber begged.

"But I lost…I have to find my glasses."

Brittany began to cry, and Amber shook her head no. "You can't. We need you to protect us. What if those terrible men come back?"

Seeing the girls' distress, he relented. "Okay. It's okay. The police will be coming back soon to pick us up. When they do, you can stay with them while I go look for them."

They waited for another twenty minutes before Detective Morehead returned. The car screeched to a halt, and she jumped out of the car, excited. "You found them? You found them! Oh, Jon! This is wonderful."

"Girls, this is Detective Angie Morehead. Angie, meet Amber and Brittany," Jon said.

Angie hugged them both and checked to make sure they were okay.

"Can you wait with the girls a minute while I go back and look for my glasses?" Jon asked her.

"Sure, but don't take too long. Brittany's parents are just as anxious to get her back as you were to find Amber."

"I understand. I won't take long."

234

Jon went back inside and looked everywhere he had been, but he couldn't find them. This made him feel anxious. What if the demons came back? How would he be able to protect his family? He prayed about it. Then suddenly, he felt a calm come over him and realized that he now had to live by faith in the battle, just like everyone else.

New confidence filled him as he thought about the battle he had fought and won. *It was God's power that beat the enemy, not the glasses, or knowledge from the glasses. Still, it's odd they aren't here. I know I had them on. Maybe the demons grabbed them up.*

Suddenly, he realized that Amber was standing next to him.

"You don't need the glasses anymore. They were only for a season."

His brow wrinkled, and he looked at her with a puzzled expression. "What did you say?"

Amber blinked as though coming out of a trance. "We need to go, dad. You can always get another pair."

"No, honey, I can't, but it's okay. I don't need them any longer."

****

The next morning, Jon walked into the coffee shop and looked around at people, knowing there was more going on than the human eye could see, and he realized that life wasn't neutral. As he waited for his turn, he looked up at the statue of the three monkeys.

"Hey, Jon, regular order?"

"Just two coffees, Mark. I won't be needing the Danish anymore."

A moment later, he walked out with two containers of coffee and headed for his office. When he arrived at the porch, he looked around, half hoping that Phil would still be there. He wasn't, and rightly so. Phil had fulfilled his assignment and moved on to the next human who needed him.

Jon lifted the coffee to the heavens and said, "Thanks, Phil. To the battle."

He left it on the railing outside of the office and headed inside. After greeting Vivian and Tom, he headed back to his office before realizing that he had left his briefcase outside on the porch. With a half-hearted sigh over his forgetfulness, he returned to the porch and retrieved it. As he was about to go back inside, he turned and look at the spot where he had left the coffee. It was gone. He might have thought that someone had just helped himself to it, but in its place was a feather and note. Curious, he picked them up, pocketing the feather and reading the letter:

"You're not done, but you're not alone."

He looked heavenward, his heart filled with a faith he'd never felt before. He headed back inside.

"Hey, Vivian, Tom, what do you say we start out the day with prayer? It may even help our counseling go that much better."

Vivian and Tom exchanged glances. "That's a great idea," they both agreed.

Spirituality and counseling had now intersected.

****

When lunchtime came, Jon went to the Bookstore to see Paul. He was surprised to find not only Paul but his son as well.

"How's it going?" Jon asked the son. "I'm surprised to see that you are still here. Or…is it because you are selling the store?"

"No, I have decided to keep the bookstore, whether it makes money or not. I'll give dad a hand for a while and see if I can't help this place make some money, but either way, we'll keep it going. Dad and I had a long talk, and I now understand the ministry and the importance of keeping it going."

"I'm so glad to hear that," Jon said. He walked back to Paul, and the two of them sat down.

"I understand that Amber and Brittany are both safe and home, most likely a bit wiser for their harrowing experience," Paul said.

"Yes, thank God."

"What happened after Tom and I left?" Paul asked.

Jon told him everything. As he spoke, Paul closed his eyes. Even though he was blind, in his mind's eye, he saw the story unfold before him, even seeing the angels that Jon had not been able to see.

"I lost the glasses," Jon concluded.

"You don't need those glasses, but faith. They were only for a season."

His words shook Jon. They were almost the same words that had come out of Amber's mouth – words she did not remember saying. Had they really come from Phil?

"We are all in this together," Paul concluded.

As Jon made ready to return to work, he passed Paul's son set up an aisle display of Paul's new book. Paul grabbed one and gave Jon an autographed copy.

"Book signing party is Saturday. Got some big-name radio personality arriving to interview me about my 'astonishing, revealing new book.' "

"That's great, Paul. I'll be here with the family." He hesitated and then continued. "I have one more favor to ask."

"What is it?"

****

It was Bible Study night. Jon related the story of all that had happened to him and his family, and he thanked the group for praying for them.

They listened to his experience and studied Ephesians 5 together. The group, too, had changed with a little less kidding around and a little more serious about the battle for their souls, kids, marriages, and lives.

Paul was also there. They listened raptly as he shared his experiences and gave them each a copy of his book. Everyone was captivated.

****

A few days passed. Jon wanted Amber to have a chance to think about what had happened and what had led up to it before talking to her. That night, he knocked on her door.

"Come in."

He walked into his daughter's bedroom. "You mentioned earlier that you wanted to talk," he said.

She looked up from her homework and smiled. "Yes, dad, I do." She turned away from her computer and looked at him earnestly.

"I've thought a lot about what happened and what I did. I think I have grown up a lot since then. I never realized what a dangerous world it could be out there, or how evil people could be. I promise that I will never do something that stupid again. And if we have a problem or misunderstanding, I will try my very best to be reasonable and listen to you as long as you promise to listen to me, too."

"That's a deal," Jon said with a relieved smile. "However, I owe you an apology."

She looked at him, puzzled.

"I'm sorry for not praying more for you."

"I should apologize to you for not praying as well."

They hugged.

"I know we may still have a few misunderstandings along the way," Jon told her. "After all, you are a teenager. It's only natural, but if we keep our tempers and pray about it, I'm sure we can work things out."

Epilogue

Across town, there was a huge yard sale going on that encompassed the entire street. At one of the houses, a man walked up to one of their tables and examined a pair of glasses.

"Unusual frames," he said. "What's the story?"

"I wish I knew, but I don't. I found these by the warehouse where I work. It might be antique. I don't know. It could be worth something. If you like em, they're yours for $10."

"My son is a student in China, and I know he would love these frames. He collects eyeglasses with unusual frames. I think I'll get them and send them to him. This would be a great addition to his collection."

"What is your son studying?" The seller asked as he put the ten-dollar bill he was given into a small metal cash box.

"The Chinese language, he plans to be a missionary over there. Said he wants to speak better Chinese."

****

Several days later, a Chinese student walked out onto the front porch of a small fraternity house across from a college. Spotting a FedEx package, he picked it, read the name, and opened the door.

"C.J., you have a package. Looks like it's from your father."

C.J., an American, came out and opened the package on the porch. Inside were the glasses and a note from his dad. "I thought you'd like these for your collection. Who knows what story lies behind these lenses?"

C.J. slipped them on and stepped inside the foyer to look in the mirror.

"They actually look good on you, in a strange kind of way. You could just replace the lenses."

He took them off, looked at the lenses. "Believe it or not, I think they're my prescription. Maybe they were meant for me."

A homeless, hunchbacked man stood nearby. He raised his tea to the college student and said in Mandarin. "To the battle."

The student put the glasses back on. The man's words were weird, but what the heck? He replied, "To the battle."

www.ingramcontent.com/pod-product-compliance
Lightning Source LLC
Chambersburg PA
CBHW050738180626
46814CB00002B/812